Born of the Soil

Kalindi Charan
Panigrahi

Translated from the Odia original *Matira Manisha*
by BIKRAM DAS

NIYOGI
BOOKS

Published by

NIYOGI BOOKS

D-78, Okhla Industrial Area, Phase-I
New Delhi-110 020, INDIA
Tel: 91-11-26816301, 49327000
Fax: 91-11-26810483, 26813830
email: niyogibooks@gmail.com
website: www.niyogibooksindia.com

Editor: Saachi Khurana
Layout Design: Shashi Bhushan Prasad
Cover Design: Misha Oberoi

ISBN: 978-93-85285-58-5
Publication: 2017

This is a work of fiction. The names, characters and incidents portrayed in it are the work of the author's imagination. Any resemblance to actual persons, living or dead, events or localities, is entirely coincidental.

Printed at: Niyogi Offset Pvt. Ltd., New Delhi, India

INTRODUCTION

It is significant that social realism formed a solid basis for Odia fiction from the very first phase of its development. The trend was set by Fakir Mohan Senapati (1843–1918), recognised as the father of the genre, through twenty of his short stories and three out of his four novels. Several novels followed the doyen's classics, but between him and works of the great novelist Gopinath Mohanty, *Matira Manisha* (1934) by Kalindi Charan Panigrahi (1901–1991) stands as a milestone and shines brilliantly as a work that gave a boost and currency to the idea of exploring aspects of realism as themes for creative fiction. Through his protagonist in *Matira Manisha*, Baraju, Kalindi Charan dared to show that, far from being an antonym of realism, idealism could serve as its *élan vital* in a most credible way.

There are several dimensions to the importance of *Matira Manisha*. To refer to only two of them, the prominently simple outline of its story proved that a novel need not be built on a complex plot in order to retain the reader's interest, if the reader could be made to feel at home with its passage—like a fellow-traveller of the characters. The magic by which the author achieves this is his sound perceptivity not only of the noble and the sufferer in his work, but also of the tormentor and the mischief-maker. Furthermore, the language of the novel is in perfect harmony with the air of its rural setting, interspersed with phrases and other idiomatic elements that infuse into the narrative a naturalness that brings the feeling of bathing in a smooth and soothing autumn flow of a rivulet passing by one's nativity.

This proves a formidable challenge for the translator. First and foremost, it demands of him—and it may sound superfluous to state—a proficiency in both languages. But that would not be sufficient to convey to the reader the spirit the novel breathes: the author's faith that true love ingrained in one's nature could irresistibly work its way into another's and inspire reciprocation in him, even without protestation by the former. What is required of the translator is something more than empathy for the characters; be he conscious of it or not, he must have empathy for the author and his milieu.

Dr Bikram Das, who has achieved the distinction of translating into English, among a few other Odia works, as difficult a modern classic as Gopinath Mohanty's *Paraja*, is evidently endowed with the aforementioned qualities. He has been commendably successful in preparing Kalindi Charan's *Matira Manisha* for its presentation to a wider readership through English. One can understand the difficulty he must have encountered in handling the original's colloquialisms, but he has tackled the problem remarkably well, without stumbling anywhere along that indispensable charm of the novel—the gracefulness of its narrative process.

Manoj Das
Sri Aurobindo Ashram
Puducherri

On Translating Matira Manisha into English

Matira Manisha, an Odia novel of a little over a hundred pages, created a sensation when it was published in 1934 but is seldom read today, so it was with some difficulty that I obtained a copy of the original text for this translation. The author, Kalindi Charan Panigrahi (1901–1991), one of the most influential Odia writers of his time, founded a school of writing called the *Sabuja Gosthi* (Green Brotherhood), whose writings came to be known as *Sabuja Sahitya* (Green Literature).

Sabuja Sahitya was a far cry from the 'green activism' of modern times, but its practitioners, inspired mostly by Tagore, moved away from the social realism of the earlier generation of writers and cultivated a kind of 'soft' romantic idealism, of which fondness for Nature was an element. Inevitably, like most young intellectuals of the time, they gravitated towards Marxism. Bhagabati Charan Panigrahi, younger brother of Kalindi Charan, is credited with having founded the Communist Party of Odisha and appears to have been the ruling ideologue.

Sabuja Sahitya had a limited shelf-life and did not produce much writing of enduring value, with the possible exception of *Matira Manisha*. Social as well as political life in Odisha came to be dominated in the 1930s by Gandhian thought and *Matira Manisha* could legitimately be described as a Gandhian text.

One contemporary Odia writer has described Fakir Mohan Senapati's *Chha Mana Atha Guntha*, Kalindi Charan Panigrahi's *Matira Manisha* and Gopinath Mohanty's *Paraja* as the three seminal texts which have helped to define modern Odia fiction. The books by Fakir Mohan and Gopinath are works of epic proportion, in comparison to which *Matira Manisha* is only a 'slight' book, in both size and range. It is a simple story simply told. That it has endured as well as it has is surprising. *Matira Manisha* demonstrates, however, that economy and simplicity in art can be as productive as creative exuberance.

This translation of *Matira Manisha* carries an introduction by Prof. Manoj Das, who is widely known and respected as a bilingual writer—one among very few—writing in English as well as Odia. Prof. Das has also translated many of his own works into English. His views on translation, therefore, have considerable significance. Moreover, as a senior writer, he is ideally placed to view *Matira Manisha* in perspective. I am grateful to him for having agreed to write an introduction to the book despite his many commitments.

Prof. Das's introduction gave rise to an interesting exchange of views on the nature of translation. Although I do not have his permission to quote him here, I am taking the liberty of reporting this exchange, as honestly and objectively as I can, since it sheds some light on a problem that all translators have to face.

Quite apart from any literary merit that *Matira Manisha* may possess, it can serve as a point of reference for students of the rural and agrarian culture of Odisha, which is fast disappearing. The language of the book is unusually rich in the vocabulary and idioms that occurred in the speech of Odia peasants of the late nineteenth and early twentieth centuries, making translation into English difficult. The technique that I chose to adopt, after some experimentation, was to leave a large number of Odia words, particularly those drawn from the rural-agrarian register, untranslated. All such words were italicised and glossed. (A comprehensive glossary is provided in a separate section of the book.)

Prof. Manoj Das felt, however, that leaving so many source-language words untranslated was not acceptable and that every Odia word for which an English equivalent was available ought to have been translated. Prof. Das also had reservations about the translation of the climactic final sentence of the original text, which has become a landmark in Odia literature, and which I propose to discuss elsewhere.

In my defence, I argued that the words which I had left untranslated carried a heavy cultural load—words such as *sindura*, *haladi*, *turani*, *dedhsura*, *diara* and so on—and were therefore irreplaceable. While some of these words (*sindura* and *haladi*, for instance) did have commonly used English equivalents, many do not have equivalents in English at all (*turani* and *dedhsura* are examples). Even when equivalents exist, they are frequently ambiguous or misleading. The word 'vermilion' (as an adjective), for instance, is explained in dictionaries as 'bright orange-red in colour'. Although several translators have used 'vermilion' as the equivalent of sindoor, the English word provides no hint of the wealth of cultural and religious symbolism packed into sindoor, which many married Hindu women wear in the parting of their hair as a sign of their *suhaag*. Likewise, 'turmeric', the alleged equivalent of *haladi*, belongs predominantly to the register of the kitchen and conveys nothing of the ritualistic or even mildly erotic meaning of *haladi*, which is a part of the pre-nuptial preparation of Hindu brides. Prof. Das conceded that such words could be retained and glossed (which is what I had done), but felt that a glossary which obliges the reader to stray even temporarily from the text is likely to be a distraction.

With great respect to Prof. Das, I feel that the unease which he may have experienced due to the presence of so many untranslated Odia words in the English text could be a reflection of the belief that a khichri of languages is a form of linguistic contamination which is best avoided in 'serious' uses of language. While it may be possible for a competent bilingual writer to separate the two languages that he or she works with, a translator finds it difficult to make the leap across culture gaps without making extensive use of the resources of the 'source' language.

I am told that the number of translations from Indian languages into English has grown exponentially in recent years. (I will confine this discussion to literary translation.) I know from personal experience that it has been extremely difficult in the past for Indian translators to find a reputed publisher who can ensure that the work reaches a pan-Indian, if not an international, readership. I had to wait for 18 years before a major publisher accepted my first translation, although it has since gone through fifteen reprints.

The reason given by publishers for their reluctance to accept translations from Indian languages has been that many of them are done in English which may not be unacceptable to native speakers of the language. Primarily, the rejection is on account of syntactic deviations from native-speaker standards, but deviations in idiomatic usage are just as firmly rejected.

Many years ago, Walter Benjamin, the famous German theorist of translation, conjectured that the goal for the translator of a Hindi text into German must be to produce *a Hindi text in German*. Likewise, I suppose, the translator of an Odia novel into English must strive to produce an Odia text in English—in other words, a text in which the language, though recognisably and unmistakably English, has a distinctive and uncharacteristic Odia flavour—a text which has an Odia soul inside an English body. How can one achieve this objective? In its normal, 'pukka' manifestation, the English language would tend to resist this superimposition of an alien culture. If one wanted to inject an Odia flavor into an English text, it would be necessary to 'tweak' the language in some way, to alter its basic genetic substance so as to produce a mutant. Through the ages, innovative writers have 'tweaked' the language inherited by them in different ways to produce effects that they desire—by creating new words, for example, or by giving new meanings to familiar words or even by playing around with the syntax of the language. Syntax, however, is more resistant to change than lexis or idiom. The Indian translator dare not 'monkey around' with the syntax of a language that she or he can never wholly lay claim to, so the easy solution, which many translators resort to in any case, is to make use of Indian-language words.

Thus far, debates over 'equivalence' and 'faithfulness' in translation have mostly remained confined to the linguistic level, but primary consideration has to be given to cultural elements. Translation is primarily a 'transcultural' operation; linguistic choices are determined by the underlying relationships between the source and the target culture.

But how true would it be to say that the use of untranslated words from the source language adds an extra cultural dimension to the text? Let us compare two hypothetical sentences here: (i) 'The bride's friends anointed her limbs with turmeric' and (ii) 'The bride's friends anointed her limbs with *haladi*'. Which sentence would the reader find more 'culturally transparent'? Or are they culturally equivalent?

To any Indian reader, *haladi* is infinitely more evocative than 'turmeric'. The native-speaker reader, on the other hand, may find *haladi* incomprehensible and opaque while finding 'turmeric' familiar. My point, however, is that 'turmeric' is just as likely to ring the wrong bells as the desired one. But the use of *haladi* creates space for cultural speculation and exploration. Meaning is not always conveyed through the use of words or sentences: more often than not, meanings begin to ooze through pores concealed between words. Space must be available for this leakage to take place.

Before I close, I must add a note on the concluding sentence of *Matira Manisha*, which, as I said earlier, has become a much-loved Odia classic. I sent my translation of the novel to two well-known Odia writers, in addition to Prof. Manoj Das, for their comments. Both writers told me that the first thing they did on receiving my translation by e-mail was to go to the last line; in fact, for one of my correspondents, this was the only thing that held any interest.

I had struggled long and hard with the translation of this sentence, which in Odia, reads: '*Chhi, chhi, maichia toka ta*!' The words are spoken by Baraju, the forgiving elder brother, to Chhakadi, the younger brother, who has almost brought about the division and ruin of the joint family but has now been overwhelmed by remorse.

I found the sentence untranslatable. The nearest English equivalent of *maichia* that I could think of was 'effeminate', which is considered pejorative in patriarchal societies. However, the two highly colloquial words that follow—*toka ta*—suggest deep affection. The tonal quality of this sentence, which is left incomplete, is impossible to reproduce in another language; it suggests a mixture of affection and reproach, but more than that it reflects the super-human compassion and generosity of the speaker.

In desperation, I left the sentence untranslated but provided a fairly long explanation as part of the glossary. However, all three of my correspondents, who are among the most famous living writers of Odia, felt that the sentence could not be left as it was; it *had* to be translated.

A sentence such as this presents a Catch-22 situation for the translator. I could see that the Odia sentence, if left untranslated, would mean absolutely nothing to a non-Odia reader; it might as well not be there at all. A gloss is no substitute for a translation; it can only supply extra meaning, provided some basic meaning is already available. All three correspondents gave me their suggestions for an English equivalent, but not one of these seemed satisfactory to me. I then thought of another solution: I added an English equivalent to the Odia sentence, as part of the same utterance. But it took me no more than ten minutes to realise that this was not going to work. It might have worked if Baraju had been bilingual in Odia and English, but the author had successfully created a completely monolingual Odia world.

Finally, I had to make do with the translation that appears in this book—a translation that is deeply unsatisfying even to me. It comes close to the suggestion offered by one of my correspondents, but is not even a shadow of the unborn sentence that keeps hovering through my mind.

Meanwhile, I can only ask the indulgence of my readers and hope that they will enjoy this tour through early twentieth-century rural Odisha.

ONE

Like our very own ancient sun, billions of other suns rise and set every day within this universe, and around each, like children playing a game, billions of stars and planets circle endlessly, creating night and day, and seasons, months and years. One of the smallest among them is Mother Earth, in which lies the country, smaller still, known as India. Within it lies Odisha and within that, in turn, is tiny Padhanpada, on the bank of the river Birupa, in the district of Cuttack, a village of insignificant human beings. That is where Shaama Padhan has his little hut. What is his place within the universe—an atom or a molecule? Who can tell?

Who was it that first set foot on this soil? There is no trace of him. Who first planted seed in that soil, tasted the first fruit? That only the Birupa can tell—or perhaps the sun and the moon! But today the soil smiles with plenitude of rice and straw; it has come alive with the hubbub of human voices. How many children have played in the front yard—Shaama Padhan, his father and grandfather—seven generations of Padhans! The village rings out with the laughter of farmers living on the Birupa's banks. Within the village, funeral pyres blaze; the dry sands of the Birupa are moist with the tears of widows. Who can tell how long this has gone on?

Which of Shaama Padhan's forbears first set up home in Padhanpada? History does not tell us. Kings and kingdoms have come and gone—Hindu, Muslim and Maratha. Religions have swept across the land in waves—Hinduism, Buddhism, Islam, and Christianity. But Padhanpada has retained no trace of them. It is like the *duba* grass that springs out of the soil each year; mighty trees are brought down by the storm, but the grass is unaware of their fall. That is exactly what Shaama Padhan's little mud hut is like: it has not acquired stone steps during the reign of any king; no one from this hut has ever frittered away twenty-five rupees in boisterous celebration; no one has amassed a thousand rupees from moneylending.

From the most ancient times, Padhanpada has poured out all its piety at the feet of the goddess Mangala, whose image of black granite stands guard over the village. It is she who protects the village from cholera and smallpox; her blessings are invoked at each wedding, each festival. Someone's tree refuses to bear fruit; someone's child suffers from chronic illness; someone has an evil dream; someone has a new bunch of bananas or a tender shoot of *janhi* gourd in his backyard: since time immemorial, the Mother has kept track of everything, good or ill, that happens in the village, and has listened to every prayer. For countless ages, the goddess's devotees have embellished her image with layers of *sindura* and *chua*, until there was no space for more.

That is just how ancient Padhanpada has remained—small and insignificant.

And of all the houses in the settlement, Shaama Padhan's house is the best known. So what if it has no stone steps or brick walls?

Over generations, the house has often come tumbling down. If it lasts ten years after each re-building, that is considered a long time—how long can mud walls and a straw thatch withstand rain and wind? Shaama Padhan remembered his father and elder uncle—what bull-like beings they were! When their house crumbled they clenched their teeth and got down to work, kneading the mud with tireless fingers, and in two days the house was up again, ready to brave the elements for another ten years. Shaama Padhan worked just as hard at harvest time; the house had crumbled three times during his lifetime and three times he had raised it up again.

Shaama Padhan's house was known to everyone, not for the wealth of those who lived in it, but for their human qualities. When a yogi or a beggar came to the village, people pointed out Shaama Padhan's house to him. If there was a quarrel or dispute in the village, Shaama Padhan was called; when someone was ill or in trouble, Shaama Padhan was called; if a list of the items required for a wedding was to be made up, Shaama Padhan was called. He had read the *Bhagabata*, but his education went no further. He knew nothing of the law or of medicine and was not particularly good with figures and accounts.

But no matter what the need, he was always a great help. If Nidhi, the village *baidya*, had to be summoned in the middle of the night to attend to someone who was ill, or musicians had to be found for someone's wedding procession, or the bridegroom's party had to be fed, Shaama Padhan would get busy at once. Not one cowrie's worth of profit might be involved. Would Shaama Padhan look for profit in such a task? For shame! Didn't he get enough to eat? If someone forgot to call him in time of need and he came to hear of it, he would come running and say, "What's the matter? Is Shaama Padhan dead? Such things happen in the house next door and he doesn't even get to hear of them? Shame on him!"

Somewhere in the village a quarrel had arisen between two camps. Heads were broken; two families were devastated by law suits. Shaama Padhan got into the act and intervened, holding this man by the hand, clutching that man by his feet, refusing to eat or to get up. "No," he said, "you may do all this once Shaama Padhan is dead—fight as much as you please or go to court—but not while he is alive!

"Why, you ask? How long are we going to be here, anyway, brother? Our fathers and grandfathers tilled this soil, fought over it and went, but the earth has lain just as it was! Did the one acre of land become two? So shall we go and so will our sons and grandsons, but these fields will remain. Fragments of broken pots and half-burnt logs of wood will lie on the sands of the Birupa year after year; then the floods will come and wipe away everything—not a sign will be left."

He was not a man to say one thing and hide another in his belly. Whatever he thought was right, he would speak out bluntly, even if it was to a prince; but the very next day he would lend his shoulder to prop up the falling wall of a hut. If someone's wife was going through the agony of labour, Shaama Padhan would roam through five villages looking for medicine. That was why everyone respected him; his word was like a line from the Vedas. Twenty-five men might have been echoing each other, but if Shaama Padhan said something different, it was his word that would prevail.

The woman that Shaama Padhan married was an equally noble soul. A poor farmer's daughter she might have been, but what of it? There was nothing mean about her. When anyone in the neighbourhood needed help, it was first to the Padhan house that she came, for even if there was nothing in the house, Shaama Padhan's wife would rummage through her assortment of clay pots of different sizes and find a quarter *seer* of rice, which she would tuck into the garment around her neighbour's waist, and send her away. "Daughter!" she would say, "there may be nothing in my house but if I feed your children when they are hungry, someone will feed my children in their hunger!"

Her housekeeping skills were legendary. "That old Padhan woman!" her neighbours would say. "One cannot but praise her! How many vessels she has, large and small, stashed away in that tiny store room! This one contains a *seer* of *arua* rice, that one a seer of *usna* rice; here you will find a handful of *khuda*, there a handful of *mooga*, somewhere a seer of *biri* or a seer of mustard seed! And that wrinkled old cow that she keeps in her hut—how much milk could it be giving her anyway? But that little she churns into butter and turns into ghee, which she offers to guests."

Sarada's mother would say, "Where can you find such a woman in these evil times? Her two *bohus* will still be asleep when the old lady gets up, sweeps her house and wipes it so clean that you wouldn't mind eating off the floor!"

Sebati would say, "And that's not all! That year, you remember, when our mango trees bore so much fruit that the cattle feasted on them, she made pots and pots of mango *achaar*. They were so tasty that if a pregnant woman licked one with her tongue, her appetite would come back!"

The old woman had had to appease innumerable deities, observe countless fasts, before the gods rewarded her with two sons—Baraju and Chhakadi. But she never used their names. "Have they become so great that they should have names by which people can call them?" she would say. The elder one she called *Sasu Khia* ('eater of one's own mother-in-law') while the younger was *Chagala* ('the vagabond'). These unpalatable names were supposed to protect her children from the jaws of death.[1] *(Please refer to 'Notes', under 'Glossary')*

The old woman did not look after her *bohus* the way she looked after her sons. "A woman is born to suffer," she said. "She will be beaten, scolded—and everything she must bear patiently. What need does she have for food or clothes? She must live only for her husband and her children; they are her happiness, her well-being! Why should anyone who is born a woman expect happiness?"

She herself had suffered everything in her life. How much sin must one have committed to be born a woman? It was beyond her reckoning. If her *bohus* ever got into an argument she would tell them, "A woman's life is one long story of sin! You will quarrel, fight and finally break up the home! What else could you do? Just look at your husbands! Do they ever quarrel? Isn't this home theirs as well—is it only yours?"

If she didn't pull them up occasionally, how would they live together in peace? One had her paternal home in Kantapada, the other in Narada. Were they born of the same mother, like their husbands, that they could understand each other?

But the old woman never neglected her *bohus*, unlike other mothers-in-law. They were daughters of an alien home; who would take care of them if she didn't? But that didn't mean they could be more precious to her than Baraju and Chhakadi. 'Your son first and then your deity' the proverb said. That was why someone had to place the bowl of *turani* in front of Baraju when he went he went out to the fields early in the morning; when Chhakadi went for his bath in the pond, someone had to bring him the little brass *gina* of mustard oil which he rubbed into his body, and if this wasn't done the old lady would tell her *bohus* angrily, "What are you going to do for me if you can't do this much? Did I bring you to this home so that you could lord it over me?"

Of the two, it was the younger who received more attention. This was only because she was younger; there was no other reason. He who is smallest, lacking in strength, gets a little more sympathy. And so the old lady was always watchful: had the younger *bohu* bathed, eaten, tied up her hair, anointed herself with turmeric paste? The elder *bohu* didn't like this at all; she walked the earth proudly because she had given birth to four children. Didn't she deserve the greater share of attention? And so when the old lady called out to the younger *bohu*, "Come, *bohu*, let me comb your hair; what a mess it is in!" the elder would say, "Does she have children to attend to that she must be pampered?"

The old lady would laugh and reply, "Don't forget, she is Khandei Tuni's daughter. And didn't I do as much for you? Ask yourself!"

The elder *bohu* would mutter to herself as she busied herself with household chores, "Why should anyone do anything for me? I am a poor man's daughter after all!"

Her mother-in-law would say, "What a jealous nature the elder one has! Here I have a *bohu* who is no more than a child and instead of saying, 'Come, let me tie up your hair; it's as tangled as a bale of jute!' she grumbles when I speak up for the younger one."

Like a cobra whose tail is in the snake charmer's grip, the elder *bohu* reared up her hood and hissed "Child bride? She's even younger than my daughters, Hara and Suna, isn't she? Still learning to suckle! My children may be gasping in hunger, but does anyone care to give them a bowl of *pakhala*? Why should I be keen to serve such people?"

"Why are you so jealous of your sister-in-law? She will learn whatever you teach her!"

"As if people are waiting to learn from me! Why don't *you* teach her? I haven't seen her ever following your instructions!"

The old lady would get irritated now. "What good has my teaching done you that I should try to teach her?" she said. "The two of you can do what you like! I have my patch of *saaga* and my *sajana* tree; I don't need your services!"

That little patch of greens was the old lady's sacred scripture, to be recited every morning and evening. Whenever you saw her, she would be sitting over the *saaga* patch, hunchbacked, with a *daa* in her hand, cutting away the tender tips. Trimming her *saaga* patch, telling her grandchildren stories and trying to play *murabi*—guardian—to her *bohus* was her entire life.

But the elder *bohu* had taken over many of the *murabi*'s responsibilities. It was she who managed family relationships: who should be entertained and in what manner, who should be given what, and so on. Her powers were exercised mostly over the younger *bohu*, who never spoke to her *sasu*—only listened in silence.

Cattle and other animals cannot speak; neither can a person who is dumb, and so people think they are unable to understand anything. They have to endure unwarranted punishment, to suffer injustice in silence. That was the younger *bohu*'s plight. She had to listen to everything but could never open her mouth. It was only the old *sasu* who spoke up for her occasionally. But she was too old; how much of the family's affairs could she take on? Still—the house was hers; she would grow sad, from time to time, when she thought that this house might break up one day because of her two *bohus*.

TWO

"Those stalks of paddy have been lying in the sun all morning, but will anyone move hand or foot to turn them over?" the elder *bohu* said to her mother-in-law. "As if I am the only one in this house who has a stomach to feed!"

"*Chhi*! The only talk in this house is of division—breaking up the family!"

"Yes, that's all you can think of, isn't it? It is *I* who must boil the paddy, pound the rice—and now *I* am breaking up the house! I am to blame for everything! The others are as innocent as *tulasi*."

The 'other' was the younger *bohu*. She was the only daughter of relatively well-to-do parents and had been pampered at home. The neighbours were slightly wide-eyed when they saw the dowry that she had brought. Married daughters started blaming their parents mentally while daughters-in-law hung their heads in embarrassment. Mothers-in-law, targeting their own *bohus*, said satirically, "My *bohu* may be from a poor family but her parents were as large-hearted as any landlord! They filled up my house with gold *khadus*, bangles, nose rings and head ornaments!"

If the younger *bohu* wasn't taught a few things, she would never learn and would continue to avoid people. She was new to the family. Since her in-laws lived in the same house, she had to learn the courtesies—how to come out and mingle with others, how to speak to each person and so on.

The old woman seldom interfered with the elder *bohu*. Who could surpass her in the use of barbed words? Besides, no one could deny that it was she who did most of the work in the house. The younger still behaved as if she was a new bride. She wouldn't even split a straw!

The old woman called out to her younger *bohu*, "Come here, Neti! I am applying a little *haladi* to Hara. Come and trample the stalks of paddy with your foot!"

The elder *bohu* smiled a wicked smile and said in a low voice, "Speak to her more gently, Ma."

The younger *bohu* was named Netramani ('jewel of one's eyes'). Netramani came and, with a sullen face, stirred the stalks of paddy with her foot. What could she say to her *sasu*? But when the old lady, after she had applied *haladi* to her grand-daughter, got up and walked towards the backyard, Netramani said loudly, so everyone could hear, "Why is there so much gossip about me all the time? Do I harm anyone? Then why is everyone so ready to attack me?"

The elder *bohu* got up hurriedly and went in and called her mother-in-law. "Come and listen to what that pampered *bohu* of yours is saying! And you claim she won't speak harshly even to a fly!"

The old woman came back and said to the younger *bohu*, "Be quiet, be quiet! You shouldn't talk back to your elder sister-in-law."

Netramani became quiet. After all, the house belonged to her in-laws. People would say, "It's not even a year since she arrived and just look at her!"

Netramani was quiet for the moment, but when her husband Chhakadi came she told him everything, adding salt and spice. The flames had to erupt at some time; how long could they be stifled?

Before he was married, young Chhakadi spent most of his time roaming through the village with a *gamuchha* draped across one shoulder, a southern-style gold ring in one ear and one gleaming tooth plated with gold, a *batua* with a silver clasp tucked under one arm, wearing a black waistcoat over a white shirt. In the evenings, he watched the *jatra* with his Calcutta-returned friends. When it was time for lunch, he would return home and ask for rice; if there was any delay in serving him, he would get up and smash the earthen handi. Old Shaama Padhan would tell himself, "The boy is wayward now, but once the yoke is laid across his shoulders he will learn!" But matrimony had not changed Chhakadi very much. When the old man heard Chhakadi's voice he would warn his *bohus*, "Chagala is here! Hurry up and get him something to eat or who knows what he will do!"

That day, there was a special fair in the village. It was past midnight when Chhakadi returned home, after he had gambled, taken a few rides on the merry-go-round and watched *Ramleela*. Had it been just another day, the children would have gone to sleep by sunset—but today they sat up expectantly; *Dadi* would surely bring them something from the fair. Only the youngest child had fallen asleep, but he had left instructions: he was to be woken up as soon as *Dadi* arrived. The old man and his elder son were asleep but the old lady was awake. Her son had to be fed when he returned. And how could the *bohu* seat before their *sasu* had eaten? The two little girls, Suna and Hara, were listening to the story their grandmother was telling them:

One little pond inside another
One little pond full of water;
Six elder brothers-in-law, six *saontas* (masters)
And their six wives, all *saontanis* (mistresses)
My husband will become the Golden King...

"*Bou*, hey, *Bou*!" Chhakadi's voice was heard at the door.

"Chagala is back!" the old woman said as she got up hurriedly and opened the door. Hara and Suna followed her excitedly, anxious to know what *Dadi* had brought for them. The youngest granddaughter went to wake up her brother.

Chhakadi had brought a variety of things—*kora* and *khai*, betel nuts, potatoes and onions. The old lady first put a handful of *kora* and *khai* in the children's outstretched hands — but could that satisfy them? They were all looking wide-eyed: what else had *Dadi* brought? The youngest child, now awake, came rubbing his eyes and stood beside his uncle.

Dadi, acting the *murabi*'s role, said, "Children, you've had your *kora* and *khai*—now go to bed!" But would the children listen? They were sure he must have brought some toys for them, but no one could talk about it openly.

Something that had a red colour peeped from *Dadi*'s shirt pocket. Two pairs of greedy eyes were fixed on this object, now in *Dadi*'s hand. He held it out in the lamplight. It was a little toy that looked like a duck. But what's this—the toy gave out a squeal when it was squeezed! "Who wants it?" *Dadi* asked, holding it aloft. Four pairs of arms went up and a cry rang out simultaneously from four pairs of lips, "Give it to me, *Dadi*!" But the toy was given to the youngest nephew. And then emerged, one at a time, from the bag and various pockets—toy trumpets, harmonicas that gave out seven notes and a toy that croaked like a frog!

Someone was in tears because he didn't get a trumpet, someone complained she didn't get the doll and, amid the howling and sobbing, the harmonica rang out. The hut threatened to come down at any moment!

Old Shaama Padhan was woken up from sleep. Irritated, he grumbled, "The moment he steps into the house he sets up a racket with the children! Why doesn't he go somewhere? Let him go to *Kalimati* or to Calcutta[2]—wherever he wants! But will he really go—earn some money and support me?" (*Please refer to 'Notes', under 'Glossary'*)

Poor Chhakadi! Inspired by the glamorous hair styles and steel boxes of those who had migrated to Calcutta, he had spoken many times to his father about going away. But the old man would say, "Why, is the soil of our village beginning to stink? Seven generations of our family have mingled in it. Will your earnings give this house a stone roof?" Whenever he disapproved of something Chakkadi had done or said, he would remind him of this.

After he had eaten, Chhakadi went to his own room to sleep. It was a tiny room and half of it was taken up by large sacks of *kolatha*, which was fed to the bullocks every morning. There was no bed; they slept on a tattered *kantha* spread over a straw mat. A small clay lamp, lit with *punaga* oil, burned dimly in an alcove built into the wall, which was slippery with oil slicks; the wall above it was black with soot. From the thatch hung two sheaves of paddy—invitations to the goddess Lakshmi to take up residence in the home. On one side of the room two *shikas* were hung; each contained a small earthen handi covered with a lid. In one of these, the old Padhana housewife had stowed away her precious *ambula* carefully and in the other, some mustard seeds, so old and stale that they had lost their pungency. On the earthen floor, resting on top of a plank of mango wood to keep the moisture out, were a wicker basket and an old tin box. Each time Chhakadi or his wife folded a paan for themselves, the finger used to smear lime on the paan leaf was wiped clean by rubbing it across the box, and as a result, the box had developed large white patches across its top.

Thick cobwebs hung in the corners of the room. A pair of bats flew in through the window, flapping their wings noisily. Rats burrowed busily beneath the mud floor, making a steady scraping sound. In short, the room was choked with belongings and all kinds of animals, which had very generously spared a little space for human beings! The rooms in which Baraju and old Shaama Padhan slept were in worse condition still. In Chhakadi's room you could at least find a couple of pictures of Radha and Krishna hanging on the walls, but in the other rooms all you saw was the scrapings dug up by rats and the bat droppings. Every day they were deposited without fail and cleaned up again.

Poor Chhakadi was fated to live in such miserable surroundings. What could he do? Did he have the means to provide a decent living space for himself? The family's income and expenditure were in the hands of his father and elder brother; no one bothered to ask him if he needed anything. He wasn't able even to buy a proper box for himself. His old father blocked every move: "No, you can't leave the village and go elsewhere", "You will not serve another master!" Nor did his brother ever say a word in his support. Chhakadi could only fume within himself.

As Chhakadi's wife finished her house work and walked towards her own room, her silver bracelets and anklets tinkled. She didn't look at Chhakadi or say anything to him. Spreading out the end of her sari on the floor, close to the door, she lay down. To Chhakadi this was the signal that a skirmish had taken place in the house that day.

Smiling a little, he said, "Has something happened?"

His wife did not reply. He got up, walked over to her and tried to raise her by the hand, but she shook off his hand angrily and said, "Keep that show of affection for your brother's wife and her children!"

"But why this sudden flare-up?" he asked. "Tell me what happened."

"What is there to tell? People say I'm too lazy even to dry a little paddy! They're burning with jealousy! But why should I fear anyone? Have I eaten up anyone's share? Why should anyone say I'm setting fire to this house?"

"Why didn't you tell them that?"

"Why should I say anything? The entire family will chew me up me if I speak! If you can't speak for me, why did you hold my hand and bring me here?"

Chhakadi was busy cracking betel nuts with a *gua-kati*. In a soft voice he said, "This house doesn't belong to her! She's only a member of the family—just as you are! Who's she to tell you anything?"

The younger *bohu* turned her face away and said, "You've heard everything! Why ask me?"

"Well, I want you to answer her in kind each time! If that doesn't work, I'll see what I can do! "

"Much good that will do! Didn't I tell you not even to touch her children?"

"But it was the old man who gave me money to buy toys and *kora-khai* for them! Do you think I was going to spend my own money?"

"Why, he could have given the money to someone else! There were others from the village watching the *jatra*!"

"Yes, but why ask others when someone from your own house is going?"

Unflinchingly, Chhakadi rattled off one lie after another. Would she understand if he didn't lie—after all, she was a mere woman! Brothers and sisters-in-law may quarrel but how are their children to blame? What could poor Chhakadi do? No matter how hard he tried to think of them as not his own, his mind grew restless for the children! That was why, without letting his wife know, he would sometimes hug or fondle them, buy them a toy or a little *kora* and place it stealthily in their hands, after he had warned them—if they told their *khoodi*, their aunt, anything, he would never buy another toy for them!

THREE

Life and death! Dream and awakening! Two separate worlds, but so close to each other that there is no gap between them. One of them a man may manage somehow, using all his skills, but the other is beyond him. He has to give up everything—home, wife and children, and pass from life to death. When the call comes, who can say no? Poor mortal—what is he worth, anyway?

The call had come to Shaama Padhan's house today—to the old woman first. Well, no regrets there—the old would become new again, grey hair would turn black, so why shouldn't she go? The two *bohus* were stroking her feet, the grandchildren were stroking her head; Chhakadi was reading from the *Bhagabata*.

The lamp burned feebly. A part of the room was lit up; the rest was in darkness. The lamp of life—when the oil is about to run dry, it will flicker too.

The lamp leaped into bright flame; within the house, long shadows danced. The old woman's measure was full.

Grandchildren, son and daughter-in-law, husband—they were all left behind. All attachments were broken—the house, the backyard, the patch of greens. The old woman was no more. Every home in little Padhanpada got the news. People said, if she hadn't been virtuous, would she have gone on a sacred *ekadashi* day, with the *sankha* on her wrists and the *sindura* in her hair?

No one saw Shaama Padhan cry when the old woman died. He followed the corpse a little way, scattering *khai* and cowries, and limped back home. "How much time is left to me now?" he said. "No more than six months or a year anyway. Surely I can survive that long without her!"

The old woman had gone. The world didn't change, not even by a hair's breadth. Our ancient Earth went round and round the sun, as on all other days. Water flowed down the Birupa just as it had done before—not for a moment did it pause. The fields of Padhanpada, the crops, the trees—they all remained the same.

Shaama Padhan called Baraju and said, "Son, I won't be here long, now. If you are working, you will mostly be away from home. Anything could happen at any time; I wonder if I shall even see you when it is time for me to go."

Baraju had not received much of an education. What he had learnt in the village *chatshali* wasn't enough to get him a good job beyond that of a zamindar's *gumashta*—manager—or, at best, that of a government *amina*—surveyor. He was employed as an *amina* now, after having worked as a *gumashta* for some time. His father had asked him several times to give up the job. "What need is there? We are an ordinary family; we don't need any show. Our seven generations were tillers of the soil. If we give up the plough and take up the pen, will that raise us to heaven?"

Baraju had come to realise that one who serves a master cannot at the same time be lord over someone. But then, one has to think of one's children, provide for them. Every time his father asked him to give up the job, he would say, "Yes, I am going to do it," and put it off. A job is like the shade of a palm tree—here one moment, gone the next! Who can depend on it? But he would argue with his father, "It will take only a moment to give up the job, but we must think carefully before we decide. I am able to buy some land from time to time out of my savings; that won't be possible if I give up the job."

Old Shaama Padhan laughed at his son's foolishness. "It is madness to think of amassing wealth," he said. "The proverb says: 'Why save money if your son is worthy; why save if your son is worthless.'"

"Is it a sin to amass wealth?" the son asked.

"Not just a sin—it is the greatest crime! It is burglary, my son—dacoity! Haven't you seen Hari Mishra of our own village? How many poor widows he has had to strangle in order to become rich! Is that wealth, my son? It's the hot breath of people you have robbed; it will burn you up, burn you up—reduce your world to ashes! Money earned illegally is like *halahal* poison: if even a drop of it falls somewhere it will burn the place up!"

The *amina*'s job that Baraju did yielded not a paisa more than his salary. People were surprised: "A devotee of Vishnu in the demons' country!" they said. "Who ever heard of an honest *amina*?" But Baraju was genuinely honest. He would not accept even an unripe brinjal from someone.

He said with some feeling, "Taking bribes may be a crime, but if one is satisfied with one's salary..."

"Yes, yes, I know everything, son," his father replied. "You are doing a job, earning a salary, not accepting any bribes! But where does the salary come from? Has your father horded away money somewhere? A salary is a salary, a babu is a babu, a *hakima* is a *hakima*. Whose money is it that you are flaunting? It belongs to the unwashed farmer! This *babugiri*, this *hakimi*—where does it come from? From those who have to starve for three days after they have eaten once! Factories, trains, ships, palaces—how did they come about? They have been squeezed out of the blood of the poor! Or was it a bunch of babus who came and built everything?" The old Padhana's eyes glowed red. He was panting for breath—as though crying in pain.

Baraju's blood was boiling. He said, trying to draw out his father, "Policemen, lawyers, zamindars—don't they do us any good at all?"

"Of course they do," his father replied. "They protect us from thieves, dacoits, cheats! Anyone who commits a crime gets the punishment he deserves; anyone who takes away another's land by force is tried in court. But who are these thieves and criminals? They are a part of us! We create them! All these *mohurirs*, lawyers, *hakimas*, *amalas*, policemen, peons—they exist because of our crimes! They are the curse that has come down on us for our sins! The more our sins grow the greater the increase in the number of officials! If we were clean, why would we need them? Why would we have so many prisons, so many policemen with red turbans?"

Baraju said, "But then where will *punya*—virtue—come from? You say we don't need wealth or property—we should go down on our knees and till the earth, as we have always done, and let the rich and powerful ride on our shoulders!"

The old man laughed and said, "Wealth can buy all things except one—*punya*! You can't buy a ticket to heaven! The only thing that can buy *punya* is *manisha-pania*—the quality of being human! Where that is missing, there is most sin!"

How true! Baraju had, during his own lifetime, seen the decline of human qualities with each year of service to a master, and with each decline, a corresponding increase in demonic qualities. The ordinary labourer, working on daily wages—what didn't he do to serve the world? He helped to fulfill the two greatest needs of man—those of food and clothing.

Human beings survive by drinking air—but how many times each day do they remind themselves of it? So too, the world sustains itself by drinking up the poor labourer's blood, but no one ever thinks of this.

Baraju had decided—he would give up his job. His profession for seven generations had been to hack the earth. How would his dignity suffer if he went back to it?

Within a year of the old woman's death, a call came to old Shaama Padhan. When the old man realised he had to go, he smiled faintly and told Baraju, "My time is up; now you must look after yourselves. Only one thing I have to say to you: let no hedge come up in the middle of the field and no wall arise in the middle of the hut! Be on your guard against it."

The elder *bohu* tutored her children. They went to the old man and said, "*Jeje*, tell us what you have kept for us and where you have kept it." The old man opened his eyes and looked everywhere, as though searching for someone, and then closed his eyes again. The elder granddaughter, Hara, shouted out, "*Jeje*, what have you kept for us?" The old man opened his eyes again; the sound seemed to be coming from a great distance. Chhakadi, who was kneeling by the old man's bed-side, stroking his head, told the dying man what the children were saying: did he have something to give them? The old man smiled again, pointed upwards with one finger and said, "For you, dharma, dharma!"

The eyes closed and did not open again. Sons, daughters-in-laws and grandchildren burst into sobs. When the elder son, Baraju, stepped out of the room where the corpse lay, six to eight large teardrops fell from his eyes. Wiping his eyes with his *gamuchcha*, he busied himself with the funeral rites. "It's all over!" he said. "The world is made up of life and death."

The news spread at once. It seemed as though every house in the village had lost its *murabi*. "He was a man indeed—a man in a thousand!" everyone said. "Seven hand spans of earth is what every man is entitled to. But inside the same earth we sometimes find gold. Here was a lump of gold!"

Everyone in the village knew how honest Baraju was. So they all said, "Baraju will preserve his father's reputation. He is rugged like his father—you will find him in the fields, with a piece of cloth wound round his head like a turban, from sunrise to sunset, and when he comes home he massages mustard oil into both his legs. That's what makes him so strong!"

And in fact, no one had ever known him to complain of even a headache; in scorching sun or pouring rain, in every season, he was out in the fields. At harvest time he carried across his shoulder two heavy loads of paddy, which two other men were unable to lift; when the fields had to be irrigated, four others would grow tired carrying buckets of water but he would be as firm and erect as a stone pillar.

It was for his truthfulness and honesty that people respected him most. Somebody's gold ring might be lying in the open but he wouldn't even look at it! If he owed someone even a cowrie, he would insist on paying it back. The rituals in the Jagannath temple might change, but if Baraju had given you his word, it would be kept.

But his wife was different. She was always prepared to quarrel over the smallest thing. She was so proud of being the mother of four children that her feet never touched the earth. She expected everyone to honour her. And so it was that Baraju and she often fell out.

Baraju had no time for her tantrums; he scarcely had a moment to spare, even to find out what was happening inside the house. At night, he would take a hurried bite and fall asleep at once. His wife would massage his legs after she had finished her house work. Baraju woke up at the touch and she would begin muttering in a low voice, filling him in on everything that had happened during the day—specially the things that his brother and his wife had said or done. "When my in-laws were alive, no one dared open their mouths—but now they have grown bold! And that monkey's cub of a Chhakadi has the courage to say I'm the root of all trouble! Who are you to tell me anything? How dare you! The deer challenging the tiger in his own den! Here you are, grown as fat as a buffalo, but do you do any work at all? Let the cattle eat up all the paddy, let the crops shrivel in the fields—how are you bothered? One poor man has to do all the work; he is as thin as a stick from running around the fields all day! We see you only at mealtime, the rest of the day you're roaming around the village like a bull! And that wife of yours—she won't even split a straw into two! But when there's quarrel both husband and wife are like charging tigers! And they say I'm the one who quarrels!"

But he who should have been listening and sympathising had been snoring away. The elder *bohu*'s narrative ended in disappointment.

Somebody else had been listening, however. The younger *bohu*, standing against the wall outside the room, with her ears pricked up, heard everything and told her husband: "'Elder brother, elder brother' you have been repeating—just come and listen to her! How could you think that your brother would take your side and not his wife's? All the stories that the wife has made up and a few that the husband has added! Complaints, complaints—why shouldn't you be sharing in the work? Why should you be eating when all you do is sit on your backside? As if she is the one who feeds us! It is I that must do everything in this house, from boiling the paddy to serving rice at mealtime! Well, let the wretched woman manage everything now, I am not going to move hand or foot to help!"

So many allegations! Chhakadi couldn't understand that they were mostly lies. So his brother was one thing to the people outside and another inside the home! What Hari Mishra had been saying was true then! Baraju's words were only smooth on the outside!

Baraju was much older than he—by ten years at least. People in at least five neighbouring villages knew and respected the Padhan household, but Chhakadi's name was never mentioned. After his father's death, Chhakadi found himself without an elder's protection—and, of course, his wife was always there to humiliate him.

On some days, when Chhakadi returned home after a game of cards with friends, he would find there was no milk for him. Or the vegetable curry would have been exhausted. The rice served to him would be watery. His wife would be enraged. "Do I have an army of six or nine children to share the food?" she would say to her husband. "There's just one person eating! Why can't he have a proper meal? I can't live in this house any longer—you can live here with your brother and sister-in-law if you like but I can always go back to my father's house, where at least five outsiders are fed everyday. Surely they will not let me go hungry!"

Slowly, Chhakadi was growing accustomed to the very things that used to upset him earlier. How long should he continue to be weak and effeminate and take things lying down? Natha Katei and Halu Sahu of his own village had left their brothers and set up separate homes; didn't they manage? They were better off than before! They had set up their own shops and were earning enough to maintain themselves. What had Chhakadi gained by living in his brother's shadow? But how should he go about the separation? Who would raise the question first?

FOUR

Green rice fields all around and above them, the blue sky of *ashwin*, pierced by the blazing sun. From time to time a solitary white cloud, showing off its fondness for aimless roaming, went floating against the sun, while below its shadow leaped from field to field. The villages in the distance were hidden by trees. The wind, coming alive at intervals, blew across the paddy fields. How high the sky was, how blue! It seemed to be staring down in wonder, amazed at the dexterity of man.

At places amid all this beauty could be seen, like shadows, some creatures working busily, bowed at the waist. Somewhere, a flock of cranes or a flight of parrots rose from one field to settle in another or to lose themselves in the greenery of some distant village. But the dark creatures hunched over the roots of the rice plants had no eyes for anything else. They had become one with the fields—mere objects, or daily occurrences, like the birds, the clouds and the sun. Sun or rain, winter or dew made no difference; their lives did not change, whatever the season. Ages had passed but they had not been able to provide adequate covering for their bodies; the length of the *gamuchchas* wrapped around their waists had never grown from four *haaths* to six so that they could be tucked in comfortably. They were more animal than human. Only earth—clay. The soil was their profession, from birth to death—their cradle, their bed, habitation and provider. They were men of the soil.

One among these animals was Baraju Padhan—kneeling among the rice plants, with a dirty *gamuchcha* around his waist and another wrapped around his head in a *theka*. How many Barajus had wallowed thus in the mud through the ages, with the scorching sun on their backs, providing sustenance to mankind—deprived of hope, devoid of expression; blind though they had eyes, deaf though possessing ears, dumb inspite of their tongues! They could not comprehend their own sorrow, could not speak for themselves. They were cattle among men. Let them be beaten without cause, let them be abused, let their master starve them—they would never protest.

Jadu Dalei was Baraju's neighour and kinsman. Down on his knees like the others, he was pulling out weeds from the adjoining patch. The two were busy talking. The other farmers were chatting away too, about their homes and families, about the happenings in their fields.

"Baraju Bhai, what has to happen will happen; everything is fated," Jadu said. "Last year I got a good sugarcane crop from my fields, but this year the plants are dying. I doubt if I can get back what I have spent."

"Well, there's nothing you can do," Baraju said. "We are farmers; we can only work as hard as our strength will let us work. After that, what is in our hands?"

"Is anything in our hands, Bhai? Karma is everything!" Jadu said. "Who will give you anything if it is not in your karma? When my son fell sick, how many gods did I not pray to? How many vows did I not make to Maa Mangala? But could they do anything for me? Karma is all powerful, brother; nothing else counts. Would I have any worries if my son was alive? If I could have gone to Calcutta and worked there for six months, would I be in debt to Jagu Swain or Hari Mishra?"

"If things could go according to a man's wish…" Baraju said.

"Very true, Bhai—a man's wishes are worth nothing. Karma is what matters: it can turn clay into gold, gold into clay," Jadu said, smiling faintly. "Don't you see it happening before your own eyes? Just look at Hari Mishra—what was he? But his karma was powerful!"

"Yes, Bhai. Can we say that dharma still survives? It's found only in the *Bhagabata* and the *Puranas*! Hari Mishra is a Brahmin by birth, but what sins hasn't he committed? How many homes hasn't he destroyed; how many throats hasn't he slit? Only the other day, when the *bandobast* was going on, he swore a false oath before the Settlement Officer, touching the *tulasi* beads around his neck, and took away Jena's lands illegally, in the presence of twenty-five other villagers! And see how he has prospered! When you see all this, how can you say that dharma still exists?"

Baraju Padhan shivered from the top of his head to the soles of his feet. There was no dharma! All that existed was *adharma*, sin and injustice! These were what kept the human race alive.

The strongest animal in the herd kills its own mate and young ones and devours them! Cats eat up their young. But is that what man is as well? Can one survive only by killing five others in the neigbourhood? He who is a little more powerful than others, whether it be in wealth, intelligence or might, will first look around for five poverty-stricken, starving weaklings to slaughter and devour, so that he may grow fat himself! This is what it means to be a man! The *Bhagabata* says:

Be not too particular in choosing your food,
Whatever you get is equally good.

But is that said of man or of some other creature? It was *adharma* that caused the wars of the *Ramayana* and *Mahabharata*; *adharma* caused the earth to split open. Isn't this the story of mankind?

"No, no—dharma still exists!" Baraju shouted out. "We may be sinners, but can dharma disappear from the earth? Why blame others—aren't we guilty ourselves? It was to uphold dharma that the squirrel in the *Ramayana* deposited handfuls of earth in the ocean to help build Rama's bridge to Lanka; it was for dharma that the monkeys volunteered to join Rama's army, offering themselves for destruction. Hundreds of kings gave up their homes and their loved ones to take part in the *Mahabharata* war. What sacrifices have we made? Our homes and our families are divided—son against father, brother against brother, wife against husband; so if a Hari Mishra emerges to start a war among neighbours so that he can enjoy the *ladoos*, like the monkey in the fable, why blame him? Are we as blameless as the *tulasi* plant? How will it help if you bash your head at Maa Mangala's altar; can she turn a demon into a human being? What humanity is left in us that we should criticise others?"

"No, Bhai," Jadu Dalei said, "you can't deny that one's *kapala* is supreme. Hari Mishra has a powerful karma—he is our mahajan, our zamindar, and the president of our panchayat. The police is in his hands; the *hakimas* are in his hands. All this is karma!"

"What you say is true, brother—karma is everything," said Baraju. "The rains fail and our sugarcane crops wither—that is one kind of karma. But here someone starts a fight between you and me, gets your lands entered in the records under my name, so that Hari Mishra can get the benefit. Then come the *amina*, the police, the *hakimas*, the *mohurirs*. We are left to float in bottomless seas! That is something different! Here our *kapala* is only Hari Mishra! Do you understand?"

Baraju Padhana's words seemed to spread on the wind, above the standing paddy. At a little distance, the wheels of a bullock cart which had not been oiled for ages creaked away as it rolled by slowly—*keyn kata kata, keyn kata kata*! The sound of the cartman shouting at his bullocks as he whipped them with his *panchana* was interspersed with snatches of song:

Who was in the bridegroom's procession
At Rama's wedding?
Only his brother Lakhana,
Ee, ee…

Jadu Dalei said, "Yes, Bhai—I understand everything, but your words sound a little strange. All right, Hari Mishra may be evil, but can't the lawyers and the officials do anything to help us?"

"They'll do what they like. If it helps us, that's our good luck; if not, it's our bad luck. But all these things happen because we ourselves are in the wrong."

"Yes, brother—what you've said is the truth of all truths. Bad things happen because the world is bad. But what if there is even one good man in the crowd of thieves; will he find a place?

"Yes, but ones add up to a million! If there's one good man, he can make twenty-five others good. When one flower blooms, its fragrance fills the garden! The stronger the fragrance, the further it will spread."

The *keyn katara* of the cartwheels had slowly moved away into the distance; the sounds of the cart driver shouting at his bullocks as he whipped them with his lash was fading away, although one could still hear snatches of his song:

They held the royal umbrella
Beneath the golden *bedi*
Ee, ee, ee…

Meanwhile, the elder *bohu*, having fed a handful of *pakhala* to one of her children and a fistful of *moodhi* to the other, walked slowly towards the ghat—the stone steps leading down to the pond—chewing a twig between her teeth, turning it into a brush for them. Relations between the two *jaas* were strained after the death of their mother-in-law. Neither could tolerate the other; any harsh word from either was immediately retorted to. The household chores had been distributed among the two sisters-in-law: the younger was to look after the cattle, clean out the cow shed, make cow dung cakes and dry them in the sun while the elder did the cooking and other household work. However, neither one would lift a finger to help the other: the elder sister-in-law never bothered to look at the harvested paddy drying in the yard and the younger one never went near the kitchen.

As soon as the elder *bohu* reached the ghat, her friends arrived, one by one, to join her. Scraping up handfuls of mud and sand from the bank of the pond, Mani Bou began to scrub the brass *handa* in which she did her cooking, and as she did so she looked at Hara Bou and said, "What's the matter, Hara Bou? Why are you so late today?"

"What can I tell you, Mani Bou," Hara Bou replied. "There was so much to do! I had to grind *haladi*, prepare some mustard paste for the *besara* curry I was cooking, give some *pakhala* to the elder child, some *moodhi* to the younger one..."

"But why?" Mani Bou interrupted her. "Couldn't your younger *jaa* have taken care of the children's food?"

"Oh, she!" Hara Bou snorted angrily. "She's a rich man's daughter, don't you know? She can't bear the stink that my children give out! When her husband and she are in their room together, whispering sweet words into each other's ears, they can't hear other things that are going on in the house. The pot of rice could boil over but they wouldn't come out of their room!"

"*Chhi*!" said Sharadi Ma, rinsing out her mouth after she had brushed her teeth. "Why is she always in that room with her husband? Would my ears have heard such a thing if Baraju's mother had been alive?"

"And that isn't all, you know!" Hara Bou said. "Her *dedhsura* might be sitting just outside the door, listening to every word—but inside the room, the laughter and merrymaking will go on between the younger brother and his wife. Anyone listening to them would think it was a prostitute's house!"

Nandi Pandiyani, the wife of the village priest, busy scooping up water in the palms of her two hands joined together to form a cup and raising it to the sun as an offering to the gods, commented, "Haven't you heard—this is the *Kali Kaala*, the Evil Age! There's much that you will see now, much that you will hear! I hadn't seen the world outside or seen the face of my husband until I was thirty! And now, you find *dedhsura* and *bhai bou* together in the same room! *Chhi, chhi*![3] Don't even utter such words with your tongue!" *(Please refer to 'Notes', under 'Glossary')*

Meanwhile, the younger *bohu* had walked out of the house, sensing that something was being said about her, and was listening keenly. When her husband Chhakadi returned, she reported every word that she had heard, as well as many that she had not heard. But what was poor Chhakadi to do? He did not have the courage to say anything to his elder brother.

Now it was open war between the two sisters-in-law. There were no elders to interfere; each was sovereign in her own realm. Why should either yield ground? They quarrelled when they sat down, quarrelled when they got up, quarrelled at each word. The elder was sitting on the floor when, as the younger walked past, her foot accidentally brushed against her. "*Bishtu*!" the younger *bohu* exclaimed apologetically[4], continuing to walk away, but the elder said, "Have you become so great that others are no longer visible to your eyes? Do you have to kick people with your foot when you walk?" *(Please refer to 'Notes', under 'Glossary')*

At once the younger retorted, "Can't you find a proper place to sit down? Do you have to sit blocking the way?"

"Just look at her!" the elder spat out. "She's not satisfied with kicking me! Now she has to hit out with her words too!"

"Well, why not?" the younger said. "Do I depend on someone for my food? Why shouldn't I speak?" And as the battle warmed up, the words that emerged from the lips of the two *jaas* would not have been found in any dictionary.

Baraju and Chhakadi returned home. Baraju had been working in the fields while Chhakadi had been busy watching a show put up by a team of acrobats, in a village two miles away. Both were informed of the quarrel; one received a detailed account of the younger *bohu*'s transgressions while the other was told of the elder's misdeeds. When Chhakadi learnt what had happened he said, applauding his wife's bravery, "That's the way to deal with her!" But his wife's response was unexpected. Turning her face away she said, "Keep those effeminate ways to yourself! Why should I have to listen to all kinds of insults just because I get a few morsels to eat in this house? Don't I have the means to feed myself?"

What means did she possess? She didn't know—maybe Chhakadi did. But even he did not know where his share of the joint lands were located. He said, trying to calm her, "Just be patient! Let's see what Bhai has to say!"

But she said, "Don't talk to me of your bhai and *bhauja*. I want my own separate kitchen!"

In the other room, Baraju was listening to a recitation of the younger *bohu*'s faults. It was clear to him that his silence was not going to be of avail much longer. He was tired of explaining things to his wife. Nothing had any effect. The world runs on trust; once trust is broken all relationships break down—between father and son, husband and wife, brother and brother, king and subject. There was no trust now between the two *jaas* and so the trust between the two brothers, which should have been expected, had diminished.

Having used up all his means of persuasion, Baraju said to his wife at last, "It's because you two never stop quarrelling that I keep away from the house all day, from morning to evening. It looks as though I will have to stay away at night as well."

If there was anyone in the world that Hara Bou was afraid of, it was her husband Baraju. He was totally driven by his whims: if he once decided to do something he would go ahead and do it, no matter what happened. Sometimes he wouldn't tolerate even the killing of a fly; at other times, you could weep your heart out in anguish and he just couldn't be bothered. Such was the man she had been fated to marry! Weren't there other husbands and wives? There was Chhakadi, for instance: the days weren't long enough to contain his joys; it was fried peas today, sweet jalebis tomorrow and a new sari for his wife the day after. And her own husband? You could shout and shout till you were hoarse but he wouldn't move from his place. Always pulling a long face as though someone had borrowed a hundred rupees from him which wasn't going to be returned! And on top of it, so stubborn that words couldn't describe him. Oh what a scorched fate she had!

"Yes, that's all you can do!" Hara Bou said to Baraju. "You will happily give up your own house and run away, leaving your wife and children helpless. If you don't like these family quarrels, why don't you tell us how to stop them?"

But the advice that Baraju always gave her seemed impossible to follow. He would listen to everything and then decide that it was his wife who was at fault. She was the elder—she should have been able to guide the younger *bohu*. Wasn't the elder *jaa* to blame if the quarrelling didn't stop? She had come to this house earlier as a bride; she had more experience as a *bohu*, as a housewife. Shouldn't she be able to manage the family now?

"As if she will listen if I tell her!" Hara Bou said, puffing up her cheeks.

"Well, even if she doesn't, it's still your fault, because you are the elder!" her husband replied. "If the two of you aren't getting along, that's your fault too. You are supposed to be wiser than her!"

With tears streaming from her eyes, Hara Bou said, "Yes, that's right—speak up for her, not me! What am I to you, anyway?"

Baraju tried his best to make her understand. He gave her many good examples from the Puranas—but all in vain. She was unconvinced.

Chhakadi had changed. All that he was interested in now was looking after his own interests and those of his wife. No one else existed for him. Brother and sister-in-law, niece and nephew—all had been distanced. The same brother who he had never been bold enough to face until now! The brother who had never once told him, "Chhakadi, go into the fields and harvest the paddy!" When Chhakadi went to the village fair now, he no longer returned with gifts for his nephew and niece—sweets made out of grated coconut, puffed rice sweetened with molasses, clay toys that were supposed to represent monkeys, cats and dogs—because his wife Netramani would refuse to speak to him for three days if she saw what he had brought. But when the children surrounded him and asked, "*Dadi*, what have you brought for me?" his mind became agitated for a brief moment. There was an aching within him when he remembered the days when his old mother had been alive. Where had those days gone? Sometimes he wanted to lift the children up in his arms, feeling guilty because he hadn't brought them anything, but *baap re*! Could he dare do such a thing while Netramani was in the house?

Baraju had three daughters—Hara, Suna and Moti. Being a *chasa* by caste, he felt his daughters had reached marriageable age. How much longer could he wait? The elder daughter would have to be married very soon: his wife was getting impatient. Things had to be made ready—everything from *badis* to *daal*, caskets to combs! So much to be done! The days were not long enough. But the younger *bohu* had no children. Would she be able to tolerate all this? She went about the house freely, doing other chores. Burning with hatred. Nothing could please her. From time to time Hara Bou would tell her, "Sana Bohu, grate the coconuts," or, "Grind some *dhania* for the *mohura*," as she busied herself in her own work. Her words pricked Netramani like needles. How was she concerned?

Chhakadi had been forewarned. "Beware!" his wife had threatened him. "If you are suddenly overcome by brotherly love, don't you dare come near me!" What could the poor man do? As far as he could, he kept himself aloof and quiet. But in certain things he *had* to be involved: how much *dakshina* should be given to the priest, how should the reception to the bridegroom's party be organised and so on, and Chhakadi couldn't detach himself completely from these matters. So when he was outside the house or in some place where his wife couldn't see him, he took part in these deliberations, but when he was back in the house he pretended not to know anything. Still, there was no escape for him. When he came face to face with his wife she was like a *tampa* snake with its hood raised. As soon as he entered the bedroom she would demand, "Why don't you remain here? Who has asked you to go out and become a *dalal* in matters that don't concern you?" Poor Chhakadi had no answer. In this house even a kitten was free to do what it liked, but he didn't have the freedom to relax and smile, not even in secret!

Hara's wedding was performed with due ceremony, in keeping with the family's position. She was covered with ornaments from head to foot. The wedding guests were satisfied with the feast. Baraju spent as much on the wedding as could be expected but it was the bridegroom's family that spent money lavishly. The people of Padhanpada were dazzled by the gifts showered on the bride by her in-laws: never had they seen such Berhampuri silk sarees or gold ornaments. Nothing was lacking.

Everyone was in high spirits. Nandi Pandiyani and Sharadi Bou sat down with the younger *bohu* in her room to fold paan leaves into *bidas* for the guests. Sharadi Bou asked the younger *bohu*, "Why aren't you in your new sari, Sana Bohu?" And she replied with a pout, "Why should I be wearing a new sari? Am I getting married, or is my son getting married?"

Sharadi Bou said, "Do you or your son have to get married so that you can wear a new sari? There's a wedding in the family—isn't that enough? Even the musicians receive gifts at weddings! Surely Baraju Pradhan must have bought new saris for all the members of the family! Don't tell me he forgot!"

Meanwhile, Nandi Pandiyani's roving eyes had made a thorough search of the house. Laughing, she said, "Oh no, she just likes to make a fuss, that's all. Here's her new sari!" And getting up, she pulled down a new red sari, which had been tucked away in the thatch.

Among the women of the village, Sharadi Bou had the reputation of being a *mamlatkaar*—an interfering busybody who loved to gossip. She never failed to remind the others that she had witnessed the wedding of the daughter of the *choudhury* of Jenapur—it was so magnificent that all other weddings paled into insignificance by comparison. Nobody knew the names of more kinds of gold ornaments or more varieties of saris than Sharadi Bou.

And this sari, which had been given to the younger *bohu*? How could she approve of it? Holding it between thumb and forefinger she made a quick, expert appraisal of its texture and said, "*Tch, tch*—this lifeless *godabari* sari! How long will it last?"

Nandi Pandiyani said, "It's just like the one Elder Bohu is wearing."

Gesturing to the Pandiyani to be quiet, Sharadi Bou said, "You don't understand a thing, Pandiyani! Just because such a sari was bought for the elder *bohu*, which book says a similar sari must be got for the younger *bohu* as well? What didn't the elder *bohu* get that she must be made equal to the younger *bohu* in the matter of a sari? Her daughter was married, so much money was spent, so many Berhampuri silk saris, gold ornaments were bought for her daughter. What great damage would be done if a proper sari had been bought for the younger *bohu*?

Nandi Pandiyani looked at the younger *bohu*'s face and said, "That's why she looks unhappy."

Sharadi Bou said, as though the younger *bohu* was not there at all, "The rubbish that you speak, Pandiyani! Why should the younger *bohu* be unhappy? What hasn't she worn, what hasn't she eaten? Why should a single sari make her unhappy?"

Nandi Pandiyani said, "Who can say no to that? Who doesn't know the family that she comes from? Her father is highly spoken of everywhere. Why should she be keen to wear a sari?"

The younger *bohu* felt puffed up. She said, "When my elder sister was married, such saris were given away to washerwomen and *bhandarunis*!"

"Who doesn't know that?" Sharadi Bou said, "It's the people in this house who are learning respectable ways for the first time."

Needless to say—Sharadi Bou didn't know the first thing about the younger *bohu*'s family.

FIVE

Hari Mishra was the president of the village *chowkidaari*—the committee of elders that looked after the security of the village. The president enjoyed great prestige in the village, but this position had not come to Hari Mishra easily; he had had to make heavy investments—many bags of fine rice and pots and pots of ghee had to be given away before his appointment could be confirmed. Through his own ability he had made considerable addition to the property that he had inherited: the houses and lands of several widows and destitute women had been dishonestly acquired and merged into his own property. But one person whom he could not stand was Baraju Padhan, because Baraju was a thorn in his side—a constant obstacle to the fulfillment of his plans. Hari Mishra had to sustain frequent losses on account of Baraju. Whenever there was a dispute in the village or in a neighbouring village, Baraju's intervention was sought. He would call a meeting of the panchayat and the dispute was settled quickly and smoothly. Hari Mishra's guile could not find expression; but for Baraju, he would have been amassing money from every dispute by writing false reports for both parties. People were becoming wise, thanks to Baraju's sane advice. Mishra had tried to make use of his cunning in one or two cases, but Baraju had frustrated his plans. How could Mishra tolerate such a thing?

Just look at this upstart from a *chasa* family; if someone asked him who his father was, he would find it hard to reply—and here he was, challenging Hari Mishra himself!

Mishra was sitting in the front verandah of his house, trying to remove, with a splinter of wood, a fragment of betel nut that had gotten lodged between his teeth. Just then, he saw Chhakadi walking past. "Who is that—is it Chhakadi?" he called out. "The son of our Akhei *Nani*? Come in, Chhakadi—come up to the verandah. There was a wedding in the family; how much did you spend?"

"You were there yourself, *Kakei*," Chhakadi said. "You saw everything; you know everything. Why are you asking me?"

"Heh, heh! What could we have seen? We were there only as guests. All that we were interested in was the food! Once the *khiri-pitha* was served, who cared to know what was happening?"

"Then why are you asking me?"

"Who else can I ask? You are the brother in that household; you must be handling everything. If I don't ask you, shall I ask Chinta *Hadi*, the scavenger?"

Chhakadi said, suddenly becoming grave, "My position in that house is worse than that of Chinta Hadi, *Kakei*."

"Eh, eh—what's that you say? Chinta Hadi? *Chhi, chhi*!"

"You're asking me about the expenditure? Did I get to spend anything or do I know anything?"

"Well, who else should know? This isn't right! Baraju should know better! You're his own brother! How can he do this to you?"

"It's not his fault, *Kakei*," Chhakadi said. All his anger was directed at his *bhauja*.

"What do you mean it's not Baraju's fault?" Hari Mishra said in faked righteous anger. "You're talking like a child! How can the wife be to blame? Are you trying to teach me wisdom, Chhakadi?"

"Can I dare to do that, *Kakei*? But then, Bhai..."

"Go! Go!" said Hari Mishra. "Your brother may be great in your eyes. But just ask five outsiders in this village! Let's hear what they have to say! When two brothers are living together in the same house, shouldn't both know how much money has been kept apart for the wedding, how much has been spent?"

"I don't mistrust my brother, *Kakei*," Chhakadi said emphatically, causing even Hari Mishra to pause a little. Falsehood has always bowed to the truth. Hari Mishra said, "Ram! Ram! That's not what I'm trying to say! But you know the saying:

> What you do not see with your own two eyes
> Never accept as the complete truth.

"Baraju is a good man, as everyone will tell you, but in my opinion what he has done is wrong. After all, the brother is no child. If your brother has so much trust in you, shouldn't you be giving him a little trust as well—even four annas' worth? Maybe the brother hasn't been sharing the family responsibilities as he should, but have you ever put ten rupees in his hand and said, 'Chhakadi, take these ten rupees and go and buy these things from the market,' or, 'Chhakadi, bring me some pieces of dried palm leaf on which accounts are written and let us write down the marriage accounts'? Now tell me, if he did these things, would it lead to a loss of trust or would the trust between brothers increase?"

Chhakadi replied, "No, *Kakei*, Brother did call me to look at the accounts and to buy things from the market. But I said I don't know how to do any of these things, and told him to ask someone else. Then Brother gave the money to his brother-in-law to get things from the market."

Clapping his hands together, Hari Mishra said, "There—you see what I mean? You see what is happening? If the brother doesn't do something, call in the brother-in-law! Who cares about the family prestige?"

Chhakadi did not have a tough mind—it was very soft. At last, Mishra's words began to have an effect on him. He was convinced that his place within the house as well as outside it was worth nothing. Finally he said, "All this trouble has arisen, Uncle, because we are living together in the same house. If we lived separately, each would be free to do what he liked."

"What's that? You want to live separately?" Hari Mishra said, as though he found the idea shocking. "But why? What inconvenience are you facing? This is only child's talk!"

"No, *Kakei*, not child's talk. We can no longer live together. From the outside it may look as though we are living together happily but look inside and you will find the cracks. Tell me, Uncle, when the food has been burnt on the fire, does the taste still remain?"

"All this is madness," Hari Mishra said. "You are both young—why do you want to be separated so soon? Well, I can understand—you are young, Chhakadi, no more than a child. You must be feeling the desire to live well, eat good food sometimes. You will want to mix with other people, listen to different opinions. I will help you, son; if you like, I will find a place for you in our *chowkidaari* tomorrow."

"No, *Kakei*. Nothing can happen unless we are separated."

"Heh, heh! Again that talk of separation! Who's asking you not to separate? But you're just a child? Will you be able to manage on your own?"

"Why, *Kakei*?" Chhakadi said, laughing. "If I come and sit outside your door, won't you give me a handful to eat?"

"No, no—don't say such a thing! What do you lack that you should sit outside someone's door? Whatever you achieve will be on your own! You are Shaama Padhan's son—how can you say such a thing? This is too much! You coming and sitting outside my door! Why, you are like a son to me! If you want, I'll give you three hundred rupees tomorrow. You can start your own shop, have your own business. The profits will be all yours—just return the loan amount to me, that's all. As the saying goes—where will the ghee drop? Where but in your own platter of rice! It is Shaama Padhan's son who will enjoy my wealth—no outsider! What a man Shaama Padhan was—worth remembering among a hundred names! There were twenty-five others who would have followed him blindly! And you are his son! Can my eyes bear to see Shaama Padhan's son wandering from door to door? No, no, such a thing can never be!"

The whole village knew how much Shaama Padhan detested Hari Mishra. Hari Mishra called one of the villagers and said to him, "What's this? I see your neighbour has been moving his fence onto your land. Why don't you pull his fence down?" When the fence was pulled down, his neighbor objected, naturally. Hari Mishra told the two warring neighbours, "You will have to deposit five rupees each. I will get your lands measured and decide where the fence should be put up." The ten rupees went into Hari Mishra's personal account and the fence remained where it was. Then Shaama Padhan stepped in and sorted out the whole matter, without a single paisa being spent.

Another incident. Two women went bathing in a pond. One of them returned home, found her gold earring missing from her ear and asked the other woman about it. The second woman, who had found it lying in the water, returned it to her friend. Hari Mishra heard of the incident. He went to the husband of the first woman and said, "What's all this? Don't you want me to continue as president? This is a serious matter! A gold ornament is stolen; the police should have been informed and a report filed! Your wife and you are happy that she got her earring back, but who will answer the police? They will come here tomorrow and arrest you and your wife and I will be in trouble since I am the president and the theft has taken place in my village! All because of you!"

What could the poor villager do? "All right, let us settle the matter here before the police arrive," Hari Mishra said. "No need to let them know. Ten rupees for the village chowkidaar and another ten for the temple of the village deity!"

Now, comparing the village chowkidaar to the village deity was absurd, because the two were as different as East and West, but Hari Mishra made the comparison possible because he could impersonate both the chowkidaar and the goddess! When the lamp burned bright, someone's fingers were bound to become slippery with ghee, said the proverb. "What an evil age has come upon us!" said Hari Mishra. "The poor woman is bathing and you pull her earring out of her ear! How can anyone survive in this village—people will steal the kohl from your eyes if you are not careful!"

Shaama Padhan told the villagers, "You and I can only be petty thieves because we are poor—a gourd from someone's thatch, a brinjal from somebody's backyard, that's all we can dare to steal. But the president, the zamindar and the mahajan are big time thieves—dacoits, not thieves. Right in the middle of the day they will threaten you, put the fear of the law into you and rob you of everything, turning you into a beggar! You have heard of man-eating tigers and crocodiles; well, these are man-eating men! There's nothing the law can do to them, because robbery is in their nature. You know the saying: it's the pig's nature to roll in the mud but a man's nature will change only when he is dead!

"There's the example of Hari Mishra, right before your eyes. A Brahmin by birth, but with a nature worse than a *chandaala*! When a hunter walking along a forest path sees a flock of flying birds, all he can think of is how to bring them down with his arrows; a fisherman who sees fish in a river by the wayside regrets not having his net with him. That's just what these great men are like! A poor widow has a minor son; she also has a beautiful coconut grove, just by the side of Hari Mishra's backyard. Hari Mishra has only a single thought in his mind now: how can the widow's coconut grove be merged into his yard? Someone has a tiny mango orchard, which happens to be next to Hari Mishra's huge orchard; the poor man is sick; when he dies, how can his widow not sell the orchard to Mishra?

"Not one person will survive in this village if he has his way!" Shaama Padhan said. "May all lands, all orchards, all homesteads come to Hari Mishra and may every man in the village become a *mulia* at his door—that is his only wish, the only thought playing in his head! Could a man-eating tiger be more terrible?

"People say it is we poor people who are thieves, rogues, devils—it is we who spoil the rich people! But is it the bird that spoils the hunter; is it the fish that corrupts the fisherman? We only take cattle to graze, but the Hari Mishras of this world take human beings to graze! We are innocent creatures—neither human beings nor cattle! Beat us with canes and we shall never cry out! How can we spoil such brainy people as Hari Mishra? Can there be any truth in such allegations?"

Such was the friendship between Hari Mishra and Shaama Padhan! And now Shaama Padhan was dead and his son Baraju Padhan had taken his place. If his cheeks were squeezed, milk would squirt out of them! How dare he play games with Mishra!

SIX

Baraju found the family quarrel growing more bitter everyday. There was not a moment's peace in the house. House? It was worse than a cremation ground! Like crows and vultures, jackals and dogs fighting over a corpse, the members of the family quarrelled endlessly. One couldn't sit in peace for a moment. Within the house, Chhakadi still showed Baraju the respect due to an elder brother, but behind his back he had begun to talk—his brother had performed his daughter's wedding but Chhakadi had been told nothing about the money that was spent, and so on! When minds are no longer united, what remains? It's like trying to knot fragments of string together!

The younger *bohu*'s complaints were growing: Hara Bou had spent so much on her daughter's wedding that the family was bankrupt; besides, how much was being spent on feeding her three other children? But since the younger *bohu* had no children there was no one for whom she could claim a share; how much could she consume alone? But Hara Bou was not one to accept defeat quietly—she was ready to take on five others such as the younger *bohu*!

What was to be done? How could peace be brought back to the house? Baraju couldn't think of a way. Should the brothers separate? Well, people did survive after they had separated! If separation restored peace to the family it couldn't be such a bad thing. Why should people cling to each other and live in confusion, like animals? When minds could not meet, what objection could there be to people living separately? It was one thing to separate while minds were still united, and quite another to separate when they were divided. Chhakadi and Baraju would be separated. Chhakadi separated from him? *Chhi*, *chhi*, how could he even think of it? A mere child! It seemed like yesterday—Baraju had carried Chhakadi around the village in his arms. Calming him when he went into one of his crying fits. The lad could be just as difficult today! Could Baraju no longer bring him around? When Chhakadi was a child in his arms, crying bitterly, Baraju would do all kinds of things to make him stop—point at a tree, a crow, and say, "Look, look ! See what's there!" And distracted, Chhakadi would stop crying. Had Baraju lost those skills? He remembered his father's words: "The boy is immature. Let no wall come up in the middle of the house and let there be no hedge in the middle of the field." Four large teardrops trickled out of his eyes. No one had seen him weep more copiously.

And now, would he be separated from that Chhakadi? Divide up the cattle, the fields, the utensils in the house into two equal halves? Could he face anyone in the village again? Baraju separated from Chhakadi! *Chhi*! Was this his *manisha pania*—his love of humanity?

All kinds of thoughts came to Baraju's mind. He was confused. How many family disputes had he not helped to resolve through the panchayat? And he was unable to solve a problem arising in his own house? It was the two women who were fanning the flames; Chhakadi hadn't said a word to him so far. Should he call Chhakadi and speak to him? *Chhi*, Baraju! How could he talk to the child about this shameful thing?

He saw that everyone was to blame—his wife, brother, sister-in-law, and he himself! He most of all. Because he was the *murabi* in the family. The house was on fire, but what had he done to put out the flames? Sitting there as still and unmoving as a tree wouldn't help—if he didn't do something, it would be his fault. If the house broke up, the disgrace would be his.

Now Chhakadi had begun to interfere in the quarrel and to use foul language to abuse his sister-in-law. Three times he had raised a hand to strike. Well, let it pass—if Baraju didn't show tolerance, who would?

But when everything was said, it was the pair of women who were responsible for letting the quarrel grow. If they kept quiet, would Chhakadi speak up in what was essentially a scuffle between women? But of the two women, who was more to blame? There was no way of knowing. But one thing was certain—neither of the two was the lesser! If one showed a little restraint the other would automatically grow quiet. Could you clap with just one hand?

Very well then—if Hara Bou, the elder of the two, could be made to restrain herself, the quarrelling would end. And who could make this happen? Who but Baraju! If one couldn't bring one's own wife back to the right path, what kind of man was he? Baraju's mind became lighter. He had found a way at last. Would he not be able to reform his wife?

That day Baraju said to Hara Bou, "There's something I have to say to you." Baraju had something to say to his wife! Which god had smiled at her today? Hara Bou's heart was swollen with joy. Anointing herself with oil and *haladi* so that her fair-complexioned body looked even brighter, she combed her hair with care, applied *sindura* to the parting of her hair and sat waiting eagerly for her husband's coming. When was it that Baraju had last spoken to her in private? Whenever she saw him, his face looked as expressionless as a pumpkin; she scarcely ever had the luxury of a prolonged conversation with him. And today the same Baraju had expressed a desire to speak to her! What luck!

But when he came to her she was unable to speak. She could only stare at him.

Baraju began, "Tell me, is this quarrel inside the house ever going to end?"

"Well, you tell me how to end it," she said. "Do I begin these quarrels or is it she?" Hara Bou had a long-standing grievance: her husband always took the side of his brother and sister-in-law and blamed her for the unrest.

"If we try to decide who is responsible, the quarrel will never end," Baraju said.

"I don't care whether it ends or not—but one thing I know. She and I cannot live together!" she said.

"Are you saying we must separate?" he said.

"Separate or live together—as you wish. But I can't put up with her temper and her foul tongue any longer."

Baraju saw that his wife was crushed beneath the burden of her own pride; it wouldn't be easy for her to shake it off. It was obvious that she was determined to separate, although she hadn't said so openly. She couldn't dare say it in Baraju's presence. Annoyed, Baraju said, "Look, I don't know how to play with words. Tell me clearly..." His lips shook; his eyes were glowing in anger. Hara Bou was frightened when she saw him in such a mood. What a man she had been married to; who knew what he would do next?

Pulling herself together, she stopped crying and said, "Why are you so upset? There's nothing the matter. I *am* looking after everything in the house."

Baraju was enraged again. "Lying to me again? You are looking after everything? The younger *bohu* is doing nothing at all?"

Hara Bou knew her tears and her howling were going to be futile. Baraju's chest was as hard as steel: nothing would melt it. Her excuses would only make him flare up again. Once, in the past, he had refused food for two days because she had lied to him—as though she was the only one in the world who lied! What lies didn't people tell?

She said in a subdued voice, "Very well—maybe she *has* been doing her share of the work. But why should she be cursing my children all the time? How have they harmed her?"

"If she has been cursing the children, her curses don't seem to be doing them any harm!" he said.

This was too much for Hara Bou. Why should the younger *bohu* say anything to her children? "Don't try to teach me!" she told her husband. "I don't need your teaching! I'll take my children and live separately."

"All right, then. You can live separately with your children. But don't expect anything of me."

God! The man had no attachment even to his own children!

"Yes, what else can one expect?" she said. "That's your last weapon to frighten me with, isn't it?" She burst into tears.

He was as immovable as a mountain. There was no trace of softness in his words. "Listen," he said, "Tears and angry words cannot end a quarrel."

"This quarrel will never end," she said. Her voice was firm.

"Very well then," he said. "Quarrel to your heart's content!"

Baraju walked out of the house quietly, with his head bowed, saying not a word. Like an obedient pupil walking away from his teacher.

It was only after he had left that she realised what had happened. Only the mother of the deaf child can understand his signals.

"It's all over!" she said in horror. "Oh God, what have I done? I should at least have given the poor man some food before he left!

He has been wandering from one field to another all morning—unwashed, unbathed!" Tears flowed from her eyes in a stream.

"How happy I was when he said he wanted to talk to me! Was it for this? So that in the end he would leave me and walk away? I tried so hard to be on my guard when I was speaking—but nothing worked. Oh, why didn't death come to me?"

This constant bickering, without rhyme or reason. Whose mind wouldn't turn bitter? Hara Bou's anger was focused entirely on her *jaa* Netramani and her *diara* Chhakadi. It was because of these two that she was unable to talk freely. Baraju and she, as the elders in the family, were weighed down with responsibilities. No one tried to understand another's mind in this house. Any word spoken by one was like poison to the others. Oh, why did this have to happen? She felt as though a mountain was bearing down on her.

Someone must have done something—surely, surely, surely! Without a doubt, the younger *bohu* must have got someone to cast a spell! Who else would do such a thing? All right, all right—Hara Bou was not going to be subdued by such paltry things. If she didn't hit back, she wasn't the daughter of Ghana Parida!

"*Alo* Moti, *Alo* Suna," she called out to her two younger daughters, "will you see where your father has gone?"

Moti and Suna looked everywhere for their father. He was lying, stretched out flat, on the stone slab in front of the village deity, Maa Mangala. There was not even a *gamuchcha* spread out under him. Nearby was a clump of thorny *kia* bushes and next to it a *kusuma* tree, on which a yellow-and-black *kajalpati* hopped from branch to branch. Baraju's field of sugarcane, newly in fruit, lay beyond. From time to time, when Baraju awoke briefly from his sleep, he would look fondly at the standing crops in his fields. They were the fruit of all his hopes, all his worries, all his sweat!

The evening shadows grew longer. Everyone in the family had gone without food. The children had been wandering in the sun all day and their faces looked parched and dark. Finally, in the evening, Baraju returned home, holding the hands of his two daughters.

What was the way out? If he didn't eat, no one else in the family would eat, and he didn't like to keep them in hunger. What was to be done then? How long could they all remain hungry? But if Baraju shied away from hunger, how would he achieve the goal that he had set himself? How many people in this country had undertaken the most severe *tapasya* in order to attain a desired end? They had subsisted on the leaves of trees. If Baraju allowed this situation to conquer him, if Hara Bou came out victorious and unrepentant from each day of fasting, how would peace ever be restored to the house? Even if they decided to separate, would the decision have been taken calmly, rationally?

Should one separate merely because one finds it difficult to get along with someone, because one feels convinced that somebody's evil nature cannot be reformed? But within the same human being you can find both good and evil, both a god and a demon. The two are always in conflict; sometimes it is the evil that triumphs, sometimes the good. When the good in a person is victorious, he is worshipped as a god; he becomes immortal and is able to influence ten others. When the evil is dominant, he becomes a thief, a dacoit. Why do we find quarrels and disputes in every village, every home now? It's because evil has become more powerful; demonic powers prevail over the godly! The wars between the *devatas* and the rakshasas depicted in the *Ramayana* and the *Mahabharata* represent the same conflict between good and evil—it is an unending battle.

Could Baraju submit to these evil powers knowingly? Would he allow evil to prevail in his own home just because he was pained by Hara Bou's tears and her fasting? No, he would not accept defeat so easily. It was for the sake of this war that Ramchandra—a king's son—gave up his home and his wife. If one was led only by feelings of affection, one would have to give up the path of righteousness. What sorrows did the five Pandavas not face? Every *purana* contains this one truth—victory to the gods and the destruction of the demons!

Baraju's own home had been taken over by demons. The same demons had invaded Baraju, Chhakadi, the two *bohus*—everyone! It was to gain victory over these demons that Ramchandra suffered the grief of his father's death, that the five Pandavas gave up their kingdom and Draupadi endured the pains of the forest! And Baraju—what was he worth—could he not put up with a little suffering? How did it matter if Hara Bou went to sleep on an empty stomach for five days, if the children cried out in hunger? Was this reason enough for him to give up the path of righteousness? Could he do such a thing? Didn't he love his own wife? Of course he did! But it was the virtue in her, her good qualities, that he loved—how could he love her shortcomings? That would not be love; it would be something less worthy! Baraju *wanted* to love his wife; he wanted her to be full of all good qualities; he wanted her to be rid of all impurities. When you truly loved someone, you thought only of her welfare. If Hara Bou was unable to understand what was good for her and what was undesirable, was it not Baraju's duty to help her understand?

But to help Hara Bou realise that what she was doing was not right, he would have to oppose her. There would be differences between them—unhappiness and strife. Well, so what? Hara Bou would not like what he was doing—but which patient liked the taste of the bitter medicine that she was forced to swallow? She might not like its taste today—but tomorrow, when she was cured, when she was well again, she would appreciate it.

Baraju reached his home and sat down to eat. His mind was not on the food. There was a constant turmoil inside his head—how could this quarrel be ended? It was so frustrating! What was it that a man could not do? Huge empires had been managed—and here he was, unable to ensure peace in a household containing four people!

Hara Bou saw how distracted Baraju was, how detached from his surroundings. He was not there in the home; he was not with the children; he had removed himself from everyone. She looked at the platter of rice she had laid before him; he had not touched the food. Greatly agitated, she said, "The man is neither eating nor drinking anything, only roaming around without a moment's peace. Which barren, childless demoness has cast a spell on him, I wonder!"

And in a flash the younger *bohu* emerged from her own room. "What did you say, you eater of your own husband?" she shouted.

Baraju was about to lie down on the floor, but now he got up and walked out of the house without a word. He did not come back. One day passed, then two; five days passed but Baraju did not return. Hara Bou sent out several people to look for him, but he was nowhere to be found.

Sharadi Bou walked in one day and said, "What's this, Hara Bou? You haven't eaten or slept for days; you look as shrivelled as a piece of dried fish. How could Baraju do such a thing? He was such a good man!"

"Well, even the best of people are turning out to be bad for me. That's just my luck, Sister!" Hara Bou replied, with tears in her eyes.

"*Chhi*, Hara Bou!" Sharadi Bou said. "Don't cry! He will surely come back."

Hara Bou's sobs were unending. "I don't know why I am still alive," she cried. "I should be dead! Will he come back to me? I have no hopes!" Tears flowed from her eyes in torrents. The children howled. The child in her lap, seeing his mother weep, said, "Mother is crying!" and began to weep himself.

Sharadi Bou said, "Hara Bou, the children are crying; calm them down. You are a mature person—if you don't control yourself, who will take care of the children?"

Hara couldn't believe it—would Baraju really come back? She had tried her best to keep her mouth shut—but that wretched tongue of hers! Oh, it would have been better if she had swallowed some *kaniara* seeds and killed herself!

Sharadi Bou said, "Hara Bou, calm yourself! I have understood what is happening here! Why would a normal person behave in this way—leave his wife and children, his home? There is something else behind this!"

Hara Bou, who was a little more calm now, said, "That is just what I was trying to say, sister, when he got up and walked out!"

Bending close to Hara Bou's ear Sharadi Bou said in a low voice, "Magic spells can be countered, you know! I've seen so many *gunias*; is there anyone who can defeat Sania Ojha's magic? Jagu Sau hadn't returned home for eight years—hadn't even given any one news of his whereabouts. But Sania Ojha produced such powerful magic that within two days Jagu Sau was back in his home!"

"Yes, but where's Sania Ojha and where am I!" said Hara Bou. "What do I know of all this?"

"But why—is anyone asking you to go anywhere or to spend a lot of money?" Sharadi Bou said. "All you'll need are seven rice *pithas* that have not been turned over on the griddle, seven lamps filled with ghee, seven tufts of *duba* grass..."

And having given Hara Bou the details of all the expenditure involved, Sharadi Bou collected the money from her and left.

SEVEN

Evening came to tiny Padhanpada as on other days. Cattle returned home; birds flew back to their nests. In the middle of a field someone was shouting, "Nabina! Come here at once!" In a *chasa* home the *bohu* lit a lamp and placed it at the foot of the altar on which the sacred *tulasi* plant grew, as part of the evening ritual. Smoke rose lazily from the thatched roofs of houses.

Chhakadi Padhan had set up a shop on the front verandah of his house—a tiny shop where paan, betel nuts, tobacco and other groceries were sold. Customers were hurriedly buying their requirements before darkness fell.

"Hey, Chhakadi, give me a seer of rice!" someone said.

"One seer for me!" another shouted.

"I want a piece of dry tobacco leaf!" a third customer demanded.

"Chhakadi, pass me that box of matches!"

"Hurry up, Chhakadi! My child is crying at home!"

"How does it matter to me if your child is crying or dying of hunger?" Chhakadi said, flustered by the rush of customers.

"What's that you say?" another customer said. "Coming to your shop was a mistake! Quick, give me the ghee and return my seer of rice to me."

"Go, take back your seer of rice!"

"Why don't you give me what I'm asking? How much time are you wasting?"

"What kind of tobacco leaves have you given me? They aren't fresh!"

"Chhakadi—two *bidis*, quick. I have to feed my bullocks!"

"Do I have four hands? Oh, how much one has to chatter in dealing with these customers! My voice has gone hoarse! Sania Ma, what is it you want?"

"Can't you hear me? Some tobacco leaves!"

Chhakadi flung away the pair of scales he had been using to weigh out rice for a customer, stood up erect and said, "Why don't *you* take over? Come and weigh these things!"

Poor Chhakadi! He had found the slush and mud of the rice fields too much for him and started a grocery shop. Baraju gave him some money each month for his personal expenses; when he heard Chhakadi wanted to start a shop, he gave him some more money. "He has been sitting idle at home; let him do something at least," Baraju thought. Chhakadi earned a little money from the shop but most of it was spent on his wife's paan and betel nuts. Initially, Baraju's children bought some of the family's requirements from the shop but Hara Bou had prohibited any purchase from Chhakadi's shop. "Why!" she told her children. "We can get what we want from Sidhi Sahu's shop! When did this couple learn how to run a business?"

Far from making a profit, Chhakadi was not able even to recover the money that had been invested in the shop. But he had to keep it going; what else could he do?

An old woman walked upto the shop and said, "Chhakadi, give me a quarter *seer* of *gooda*. I am making *arisha pitha* for my grandchildren and there is no *gooda* in the house."

"There is no *gooda* in the shop either, Bhalu Maa," Chhakadi said. "Uday Rout bought a seer yesterday and I don't have any more."

"What will I give my son for breakfast tomorrow morning then?" the old woman grumbled. "He likes *chooda* and *gooda* for breakfast!"

Sugarcane was an important crop in Padhanpada and Baraju himself grew sugarcane on two acres of his land. When the cane was mature, farmers carried it in bullock carts to the crushers, about a mile away. The cane was crushed and the juice boiled in enormous vats over open wood fires. After about five hours of boiling the sugarcane juice was reduced to a thick brown sticky mass—*gooda* or molasses, loved by villagers, which formed a staple food. This was poured out into round moulds and left to dry in the sun for about a week. When it had solidified into rock-hard, concrete-like slabs, the *gooda* was prised out of the moulds and stored away. Every farmer of any substance had in his house numerous slabs of *gooda*—the fruit of several harvests.

Most of those who visited Chhakadi's shop came not to buy, but to gossip and chat. Genuine customers made their purchases early and returned to their homes; thereafter, it was time for the idlers and gossip mongers. Sometimes Hari Mishra put in an appearance too. Baraju was his prime target. "Let the two brothers separate; let the quarrel between them grow," he said to himself. "Baraju goes round the village claiming he can settle every dispute; let us see if he can deal with the quarrel in his own home!"

"What news, prince?" Hari Mishra said to Chhakadi tauntingly. "How is your shop doing?" Chhakadi promptly spread out a mat on the verandah, invited Hari Mishra to sit down and offered him a paan.

Hari Mishra went on, "You did well to start this shop. You couldn't have managed the fields."

Another of the gossipers, Dharamu Das, said, "It was because some of us kept on badgering him that he started the shop; otherwise, who is Chhakadi Padhan and who is a shop?"

Hari Mishra had a bad squint. He would be sitting chatting to a group of ten and each person in the group would think that Mishra was looking at him. When he was looking straight ahead his eyes were turned slightly to the right and when he was looking to the left he seemed to be looking straight ahead. Now, looking slightly to Dharamu's left, Mishra said, "What nonsense! Was it somebody else's father who helped Chhakadi to set up the shop? The father had left money behind and so the son started a shop."

Chhakadi said, "No, *Kakei*, my father had not left a paisa behind. When he was dying he told us, 'All I am leaving behind for you is my dharma.'"

"Oh yes, I have heard all that," Hari Mishra said. "The old man and his wife had left nothing behind; it was Baraju Padhan who poured all the money at your feet out of his own earnings so you could start the shop. Who will believe that?"

"I can't answer that, *Kakei*. Both of them died before my eyes, but if they left some money behind I don't know about it," Chhakadi said.

"Heh, heh! How could you have known?" Hari Mishra said. "You were either completely innocent or completely ignorant at the time. You know the saying, don't you: 'How much does a seer of rice cost?' 'I don't know, I have all my meals in the *mattha*.' Isn't that right, Dharamu?"

"No, *Agnya*," Dharamu said. "It was Baraju who gave his brother the money. He had to take a loan from Guna Parida."

"Oh, don't try to teach me wisdom," Hari Mishra said. "I knew both Shaama Padhan and his wife and I've known Baraju since he was a child."

"But *Agnya*," Dharamu protested, "we have never heard anything against Baraju."

"Keep quiet, will you?" Hari Mishra said sternly. "How dare you contradict me? What do you know, anyway? Don't talk big! What do you say, Chhakadi?"

"You are right, *Kakei*. People say the plans of 'Nara', the ordinary mortal, are unknown even to 'Narayan', God."

"Did you hear that, Dharamu? Only a wise person can understand these things! Dharamu Bauri, the *mamlatkaar*, will talk big because he knows nothing. He is the kind of man who gets up in the morning and rushes off at once to his fields with his plough across his shoulder, while his bowl of *turani* grows as cold as ice. And that Dharamu Das is sitting here, talking to us as an equal! That's what the world has come to; small people have acquired big mouths."

Dharamu was shrinking within himself. "No, *Agnya*," he said to Hari Mishra. "Do I dare contradict your words?" He used the more intimate form *tuma*, although he had intended to elevate Hari Mishra to the highest honorific level; the Odia pronoun *apana* was not a part of his vocabulary.

"Keep quiet, stupid!" Hari Mishra said. "All right. Let us accept that it was Baraju Padhan who gave Chhakadi the money for this shop. What's so great about that? He was controlling the entire property; if he gave his younger brother fifty or a hundred rupees out of the family's money, what great favour did he do him?"

Chhakadi said, "Why do you listen to Dharamu's talk, *Kakei*? What does he know about the affairs of our family?"

Dharamu Das, alias Dharamu Bauri, was known for his fondness for telling tall stories. Even if he was thrashed every day, he would not give up his habit. Although he was in no position to contradict Hari Mishra, he turned upon Chhakadi now and said heatedly, "Oh, I know how capable *you* are! That's why you are about to eat up the deity's *khatuli* after you have eaten up the deity Himself! This shop that you say you are running—will you be able even to pay back the money that Baraju gave you to start it?"

"Go! Go!" Chhakadi shouted at him. "Don't you dare talk about things that you know nothing about—not in *Kakei*'s presence."

"There's a lot of heat in your words today, Chhakadi!" Dharamu said. "Are you going to beat me up? Remember, this Dharamu is a *bauri* by caste—he owns neither land nor house; nor does he have money or gold which someone can take away from him dishonestly. Some people like to cheat others and take away all that belongs to them but how does that help? I am used to being abused and beaten since I was a child. I haven't stolen anything for which I can be jailed!"

What was this? A mere *bauri* speaking with such confidence in Hari Mishra's presence! But then Dharamu was known for talking out of turn—Hari Mishra had beaten him up enough times to be sure about this. He glared angrily at Dharamu and said, "Your back is itching for another thrashing, isn't it?"

What did Dharamu stand to lose? They would take turns to beat him up; he was so used to this that he had no fear now. Even then, he wasn't keen to receive another thrashing in the middle of the night. He got up and prepared to walk away, saying, "Yes, yes—that's the only threat you big people can hold out! You will either take turns to beat me or drive me out of the village. I am just a poor peasant; as long as there is strength in my arms, my belly will not remain empty. But the wealth that you are trying to grab from others—even a gourd growing on someone's thatch is not safe from you—will that remain? I'm not worried for myself—I can always find work in some other village if not here."

"All right, that's enough!" Hari Mishra said. "Go now! It's late in the evening and if I give you the thrashing that you deserve, I'll get polluted and will have to bathe again! I'll take care of you tomorrow!"

"Haven't you done that ten times already? What is new?" Dharamu said.

"Do you see what is happening, Chhakadi?" Hari Mishra said when Dharamu had gone. "You see how bold these small people have become? And who is responsible for this? Who but your brother Baraju! If he goes and sits with these *dombs* and *bauris*, teaches them wrong things, what else can one expect? You remember the court case in which Ghana Khatei of our village was involved, don't you? Baraju went around the village instigating everyone and telling them the case was false, and the result was that I couldn't find a single witness to support us. Are you the only truthful man in the whole world? And is everyone else a liar? Now you tell me, Chhakadi, who doesn't have to tell a lie now and then? Who has a bone inside his tongue?"

"But *Kakei*, everyone in the village says my brother never tells a lie."

"Oh yes, he can throw dust in the eyes of fools but you and I know the truth! And surely you can see what is going on in your own house—you may be saying one thing while your wife says another!"

"Yes, *Kakei*, I know everything; I don't need to be taught by Dharamu Bauri. You heard what he said about me? I am eating up the deity's *khatuli* after devouring the deity!"

"Oh, he! It was lucky for him I wasn't in the mood to bathe again in the evening or I would have taught him the lesson of his life!"

Chhakadi had been deeply offended by Dharamu's words. He would have been happy if Dharamu had been thrashed. Taking advantage of Hari Mishra's support, he said, "We will have to give him a sound thrashing tomorrow morning, *Kakei*. Things have gone too far!" The mere thought was pleasing to him.

"You don't have to remind me, Chhakadi," Hari Mishra said. "Just walk over to my house early in the morning. Dharamu cannot be dealt with in the usual way; he needs some special treatment—a *pagha* that you tie bullocks to, a coconut tree and a *bichchuati* plant, that's what we will need to fix him. But Dharamu is not the real problem—he can be fixed in an hour, but how do we cope with your brother,

Baraju? We may deal with one Dharamu today but tomorrow three others will come out naked to fight us at your brother's teaching! Is there a way to deal with him? Just look at him—teaching a low-caste *bauri* to insult his own brother! Dharamu is just an illiterate fool; how would he know that you have eaten up the deity and are about to eat up the deity's *khatuli*—that your shop is sunk in debt and litigation? Chhakadi, don't try to tell me Baraju is not behind all this!"

"I have understood everything, *Kakei*, although I should have been listening more to my wife," Chhakadi said. "But there's a lot of truth in what women say in the house. She has been telling me for a long time—let us get our own kitchen. There are three daughters to be married—the expenses will come out of the family money, where else? Why should *we* get involved; why should we work so hard to feed strangers?"

As soon as he uttered the word 'strangers', Chhakadi experienced an odd feeling within him—yes, what were they if not strangers; were they his own? Wasn't the family divided already; wasn't each person looking after his own interests? Chhakadi was getting his paan, betel nuts and *gundi* from his own shop while Baraju bought these things elsewhere. Friendly talk between the two *jaas* had become a dream; they spoke only to quarrel. Was there any understanding between them? It was the elder brother who managed the home and had charge of the money; had he ever tried to involve Chhakadi in family matters? When there was so much division inside, why try to appear united from the outside?

Finding an opportunity, Hari Mishra said, "Chhakadi, you spoke about women's talk, but remember, a woman is the Lakshmi of the house! What do we men know of what is happening in the house? We are only seen outside, but it is the women who manage everything—fetch everything that the home needs. It is idiots like Dharamu Das who will talk disparagingly of 'womanly talk'. Why should one listen to such people? My wife—Basu's mother—had been telling me for ages that we should divide up the family home, but I never listened because it was only 'womanly talk'. But since the day my brother and I separated, God has been looking after me in joy and sorrow. Or have I been running from Calcutta to Medinipur like my brother Kela, to work as a cook in the homes of Bengali babus or to go begging from door to door?"

"Why, *Kakei*, why do you say such things? Why should you have to beg? What are we there for?"

"Heh, heh! Just a child, unable to understand things! What need is there for *you* to beg? You own ten acres of land, a plough, bullocks...a home that goes back seven generations. But whatever you may say, Chhakadi, all this is happening because of your own incompetence!"

"*Kakei*, you know one needs experience to become a farmer. Does anyone give me a chance to learn?"

Losing his temper, Hari Mishra said loudly, "Why should anyone give you a chance? Are you a baby learning to suckle at your mother's breast?"

Chhakadi said, "No, *Kakei*, this year I'll follow Chandra Sial's advice. He advised me to set up my own *khala* in the five-acre *chaka* where we grow *mooga*, and to store the *mooga* crop there after it has been harvested. I told him, 'How can I do that? It's my brother who does all the hard work and makes the crops grow—the harvest should go to him,' but Chandra said, 'Who has been giving you this stupid advice? Don't forget, you are part owner of the land and if your brother has been cultivating it, the expenses came out of the family funds. Don't people give their land to sharecroppers? Does that mean that the man who cultivates the land should take the entire crop? No, the owner of the land gets half.' I tell you, *Kakei*, Chandra may be only a low-caste *sial*, but he has brains! When I told my wife what Chandra had said, she said, 'Do we need to ask anyone about this? Prepare your own *khala* next to the old one and that's where we will keep the *mooga*.'"

"This is the first time I've heard you say something sensible, Chhakadi," Hari Mishra said. "Yes, of course—this is the right thing to do; it won't hurt anyone's prestige. You are not setting up a separate kitchen! Your elder brother has been taking all the profits from the land for the last ten years; it's time the younger brother got his share. No one should mind; it is only what is due to you! Of course Chandra Sial is clever; he can wring water out of dry wood. It's not for nothing that I have employed him as a *piyada*."

Chandra Sial had been standing nearby, listening to the conversation. He quickly deposited his thick bamboo staff in the doorway of a shop, rushed out and prostrated himself headlong at Hari Mishra's feet. Mishra looked at his face and said, "*Arre*, it's Chandra, isn't it? You'll have a long life, Chandra; we were just talking about you. What news, Chandra?"

Chandra was Hari Mishra's constant attendant as well as confidant. He kept Mishra informed of everything—who sneezed where, who sat where, did what. Devotees of the Great God, Shiva, had to first pray to His vehicle, the Divine Bull, Brishabh; it was necessary to embrace Garuda, the Celestial Eagle who carried Vishnu on his back, before one could enter Vishnu's temple and have a glimpse of the Supreme God. So too, anyone who wished to escape the clutches of Hari Mishra was required to first placate Chandra Sial.

"*Agnya*, the news is terrific today!" Chandra said. "If you come this way, I'll tell you."

"What need is there for me to go anywhere?" Hari Mishra said. "Chhakadi is like my own son. He's not going to talk."

"*Agnya*, this is about that Sadei Barik. His son-in-law has been working in Calcutta for the last two years while his daughter is with the father. You know what happened last year—the girl disappeared and there was no trace of her. But come and see what is happening now, among the banana plants in Sadei Barik's backyard! A newly born child howling away!"

"Eh, eh, what's that you say? Is it alive?"

"Howling so loud that the banana plants are shaking! And the one who gave birth to the child is cooking rice in the kitchen—all bathed and washed! It was Sharadi Bou who gave me the news a few moments ago or else how would I have known?"

"This is really big news!" Hari Mishra said. "But you say the child is alive—if it wasn't, maybe something useful could come out of this! Anyway, go and call the chowkidaar; file a report in the police *thana*! Where is Sadei Barik?"

"What can he do now? The news has spread all over the village. But it won't be easy to tackle him; you know how cunning he is."

"Let him be anywhere—how does it matter? After rice has been parboiled, where can it go but into the *dhenki*? Go and inform the chowkidaar. Do you see what a hard life I lead, Chhakadi? Not a moment's rest! Go, my son, close your shop, eat and go to sleep. But don't neglect this old *Kakei* of yours; let me know if something happens!"

"Do you need to tell me that, *Kakei*?"

In every village, among the banana plants, among the fields of jute, among the roots of *kia* bushes, on the banks of ponds, the cries of newborn babies were heard. How difficult life could become for a human child! But did anyone try to do anything about it? The Hari Mishras beccame richer; the Sadei Bariks were harassed. Tears came to Baraju Padhan's eyes when he heard the cries of babies. But:

Those whom the gods protect
What harm can the powerful do to them?

EIGHT

Hara Bou made countless vows to her gods and goddesses: "Maa Mangala, bring back my husband safely and I'll sweep and wash your temple clean and offer you a new sari! Lord Kapaleswar, I'll bathe you with one lakh pots of consecrated water if you help my Baraju to return to me safely."

For five days no one knew where Baraju was. That was when Sharadi Bou took some money from her to obtain the services of an *ojha*, a witch doctor, and the same evening her daughter Moti came rushing into the house, eyes shining with excitement, and said, "Bou, *Bapa* is back!"

Hara Bou was sitting in the doorway, rolling cotton wicks for the lamps she would light that evening at the shrine of the family deity. The effect of Moti's announcement on her mind can only be imagined.

When Baraju came and stood in the doorway, Suna brought him a pot of water to wash his feet with. Hara Bou looked up from the task of rolling wicks and gazed at her husband's face. It looked dry and weather-beaten; his hair was ragged and it seemed he had not eaten for some days. She quickly got up and walked into her own room, weeping like a child, her tears flowing uncontrollably.

Baraju was back but his return seemed to have given him no joy. His face looked as hard and drawn as before. All he would say in reply to Hara Bou's questions was, "Yes!"

Netramani found the situation highly entertaining. Slipping the end of her sari off her head, with a broad smile playing on her paan-stained lips, she said to Chhakadi, "Watch how much fuss will be made in this house now—how much drama there will be! Just to impress us!"

Chhakadi was pleased to see his wife in high spirits. "Yes, of course," he said. "It's all being staged for our benefit; what else?"

Netramani said, "But do you know the real reason behind this drama? The marriages of Sona and Moti are drawing near. And that wretched woman knows how excited you will be over the event—how you'll forget everything and celebrate and dance in joy! But I'm warning you in advance—I am not going to be here at the time of the marriages! You will have to take me to my father's home and leave me there—is that understood?"

Poor Chhakadi was in a fix. His wife would go home again. For six months or maybe a year. Her mother would say, "My poor daughter looks so sickly; I'm not going to let her go back for at least another two months." Her father would say, "What's the hurry? Why this talk of her going back the moment she arrives? Are termites eating up the house?"

All Chhakadi could say to his wife now was, "Wait, wait, let us be patient! How can the marriages of Suna and Moti be performed if we are not here?"

Hara Bou had lost face. The entire village was saying, "Baraju left his home and ran away because he and Hara Bou couldn't get on!" Her younger *jaa* and *diara* were having fun at her expense—well, that was her fate! Hara Bou was too ashamed to show her face to neighbours. Everyone who saw her would smile and say, just to annoy her, "What's this we hear, Hara Bou? You quarrelled with Baraju so violently that the poor man had to leave home?"

Well, what had to happen had happened—Hara Bou was past caring. But she only wished the poor man could smile and talk freely again, eat happily and go round the village meeting friends and neighbours as before. How had that wretch Sharadi Bou helped? She had cheated Hara Bou of some money, but what results had she delivered?

Hara Bou talked to Baraju about many things—about the in-laws of her eldest daughter, Hara; about the marriages of Sona and Moti, which would have to be performed soon. But on no topic would Baraju talk to her freely.

Hara Bou said to her husband, "You have cut yourself away so completely from everything; will I have to look for husbands for Sona and Moti now?"

"Did I say that to you?" Baraju replied.

"Well, my daughters can't remain unmarried for ever, can they?" Hara Bou said. "We are living in this house jointly with others. Chhakadi will demand a division of the house tomorrow; plans are being made already."

Baraju said slowly, "Hara Bou, I do not wish to learn from you what plans are being made by whom."

Hara Bou's face shrank. But if she didn't talk, Baraju would say nothing. She said again, "Why are you angry? Have I done anything to lower your prestige in the village? Five days you were away from this house, lying hungry in some godforsaken place! Why? What did I do against your wishes?" Her eyes were wet.

Baraju said, "I am not asking you to act according to *my* wishes. But why don't you decide for yourself what should be done? Why don't you do that which will be best for the family?"

"Look—I am just a woman; how can we women understand these things? But you tell me—what will be best for the family?"

Baraju saw that there *had* been some change in Hara Bou. This was perhaps the right time to bring her around. He said, "Very well—there's one thing that you can do. Just don't give her an excuse to start a quarrel; don't say any harsh words to her at all. If she says something to hurt you, or says anything against me or the children, just ignore her and do not answer back. I know it will be painful; but how many painful fasts do you not observe? Just think of this as another fast that you have vowed to observe and put up with the pain. Will you do this?"

"Yes, why not?" she said, but it was clear to Baraju that she was speaking without conviction. Only two days later there was another quarrel between the sisters-in-law. Hara Bou immediately regretted what she had done and could have bitten her tongue in embarrassment. Baraju had given her so much advice; how could she have forgotten everything in her anger?

"That was a good fast you observed," Baraju teased her, but she said, "Don't make fun of me! My stupid mind can't remember anything!"

"All right, this time you forgot what you had to do. Next time, when the same thing happens again, *I'll* do what I think is best!"

Hara Bou was a little scared. God knew what he'd do! But if the younger *bohu* kept abusing and cursing her children in her presence, how long could she keep quiet?

Baraju saw that he could not change his wife's behavior by merely running away from home. He would have to remain in the house and play a more active role. If Hara Bou failed to observe the vow, he would take the vow upon himself. He would not speak inside the house at all—not to Hara Bou, not to the children, not to anybody. If he stopped speaking to Hara Bou alone, that wouldn't be very effective; she would make the children speak for her and get everything done through them!

A week or ten days passed. No matter what Netramani said or did, Hara Bou never retaliated, never replied to her, although she was itching to hit back. The younger *bohu* shouted, screamed, stormed and raved, called her names to her heart's content, inciting her to offer combat, and finally lapsed into silence. Would Hara Bou have tolerated such things usually? When Baraju was away from home she did manage to slip in a word or two sideways before she resumed her silence. It had to be done with great skill and timing because if Netramani heard her she would immediately raise the fight to the highest pitch. What if Baraju returned unexpectedly? Hara Bou's mouth was clamped shut as long as Baraju was inside the house or anywhere within hearing.

One morning, no one knows why, Baraju returned from the fields early with his plough on his shoulder. He was still at the front door, putting the plough down, when he heard voices inside the house. The dominant voice, of course, was Netramani's, but Hara Bou did interject a sentence or two from time to time, making the fire blaze out. As soon as Hara Bou saw Baraju inside the house, she put out her tongue in embarrassment and became quiet. Baraju's presence dampened her fighting spirit completely. But the younger *bohu* seemed to have given up all shame or sense of right and wrong; her voice became a little subdued on seeing Baraju but the flow of abuse did not stop.

Baraju was greatly depressed. He felt he was responsible for everything that was happening in the house. What a sinful life his was! He had lost honour and dignity; the happy home had become a chaos. Was it all going to end in disaster? Would a wall finally go up across the home, dividing brother from brother? But would that end the quarrel? The seeds of strife had entered everything: everyone would be on alert, watching each other like hawks: who threw the ashes from the hearth into the other's space, whose cat jumped across the wall...Would one of the two brothers move to a home elsewhere? If man failed to conquer the devil within him and allowed hatred and strife to grow, what would happen to society? Why would anyone require neighbours and friends? What would happen to villages and towns? Would human beings become solitary forest dwellers again?

Baraju did what he had decided to do. He completely stopped speaking within the house. If his wife asked him something or his children spoke to him, he would not even look at them. He seemed to have become not only dumb, but a little mad as well. Hara Bou could make no sense of his behavior—what was happening? How could someone not talk? She didn't know whether to laugh or cry.

One day followed another—but Baraju did not speak. Sometimes he would stare wide-eyed at others. There had been a time when he couldn't swallow a handful of rice unless there was some fish to go with it. Hara Bou would somehow manage a little *jaradi* fish or a piece of dried and salted *sukhua* for him, which she wrapped in a banana leaf and roasted over an open fire. But now Baraju had developed an aversion to fish as well as meat. He had taken a vow—how could he violate it until he had achieved his goal? Not a drop of oil had touched his skin or his hair in weeks. When Hara Bou tried to massage his feet with a little oil at night, as had been usual, he got up and walked away. In the beginning, when Baraju had given up speaking, Hara Bou had been amused and had laughed, but now his silence brought tears to her eyes.

Innumerable festivals are celebrated in the villages of Odisha. That day, it was *Chitou Uansa*, a day when housewives make *chitou pitha*—a kind of fried pancake made from rice flour and black beans. Baraju had been very fond of *chitou pitha* and so Hara Bou made some special *pithas* for him, blended with grated coconuts. She would feed her husband to her heart's content!

Baraju sat in the doorway, weaving a rope out of strands of jute fibre. His two daughters sat beside him. Just then Hara Bou came with a *thalia* full of *pithas*, bowed to Baraju in observance of the special rituals she was required to perform on that festive day, and put the *thalia* down in front of Baraju. Then, rushing back immediately to her kitchen, she returned with a small *gina* full of milk and another platter containing a *santhula* of lightly curried vegetables and a lump of jaggery. Baraju, who had barely torn off a small fragment of *pitha* and carried it to his mouth, got up, preparing to walk out of the house.

Hara Bou was unable to control herself. She burst at once into a loud sob and caught Baraju's hand tightly. "Why are you punishing me in this way?" she howled. "Eat that *pitha* and I'll do whatever you say! I'll make any vow you want me to make." Since the day her husband had stopped speaking to her, the elder *bohu* had not spoken to her younger *jaa* either. But this wasn't enough to satisfy the younger *bohu*—there were scores to be settled. The main thing was the relationship between minds: if minds remained bitter, nothing would work.

Then Baraju spoke—and the elder *bohu* felt as though all the treasures of the earth had been poured into her lap. "Shall I tell you, then?" Baraju said. "Will you do as I ask?"

"Yes—certainly, certainly, certainly! Whatever you say."

"But why can't you do it yourself, without my asking? Why can't you do what is good for this house, for all of us?"

"No, no, I know nothing; I can understand nothing!" she cried. "I'll do whatever you say!"

Meanwhile, Chhakadi and Netramani had peeped out of their room once or twice and seen what was going on. Baraju was standing, his ragged hair flying wildly, looking like a ghost while his wife—his proud wife whom nothing could bend—stood next to him, gripping his two hands in hers, with her head bowed. Seeing this drama, Chhakadi and Netramani retreated into their own room, stuffing their mouths with wads of cloth to suppress their laughter.

Baraju continued to stand there, as immovable as a mountain. "Very well then, promise me you will never, from your side, start a quarrel with the younger *bohu*!" he said.

Hara Bou's tears flowed in an unending stream from her eyes to Baraju's feet. Sobbing like a child, she said, "I promise! I'll never quarrel with her."

"No matter what others say to you, you will listen to everything quietly?"

"I will listen to everything quietly!"

"Very well. Now come with me inside the house and I will tell you what more you must do," Baraju said. His feet were damp with Hara Bou's tears, but whether those callused feet had been softened as well, only he could tell.

Hara Bou saw that she had been turned into an object of ridicule, but since it was only Baraju who had witnessed her humiliation, how did it matter? What could she hide from him? What did they not share? Outside her own private space she had worn a protective covering of pride and self-respect, but that had been blown away. Whom should she fear now? Her younger *jaa* and Chhakadi? The neighbours? She did not let go of Baraju's hand. "What is it that you are going to tell me? Say it here!" she said in a calm voice.

Baraju never felt any shame or embarrassment for himself—he was beyond such things. But how much sorrow and pain had he brought to this unlettered wife of his! She was his wife after all, the mother of his children. Every woman was an embodiment of Lakshmi, of Shakti; it was Woman who received worship as Durga. How could Baraju reduce her to such insignificance? Baraju rejoiced on seeing that Hara Bou had shed her false notions of respectability.

He said, "Hara Bou, I want you to promise me something. Whatever is cooked in this house, whatever milk or ghee we have, will be given first to Sana Bohu and Chhakadi. Then to the children, and lastly to you and me!"

Hara Bou had been listening to him with her eyes closed. "My children last of all!" she thought to herself. "Are they my children alone? If that's what he wants, so be it!" She would harden her heart.

Baraju smiled a little and said, "Hara Bou, you have held my hand and agreed to everything I said. If you don't keep your promise, it will mean that my life has no value for you."

Hara Bou had not realised that she was still holding her husband's hand. Her face grew red with embarrassment and she let go his hand at once.

Baraju sat down cross-legged on the verandah. The *thalia* containing *chitou pithas* still lay on the verandah. Baraju chatted happily with his children. Hara Bou had lost all her pride but still, when Baraju said, "Hara Bou, bring me some of that *santhula*. And a green chilly!" she felt as though someone had lifted the mountain that had lain on her breast, crushing her under its weight. In the *Ramayana*, Ahalya was turned into a stone image under her husband's curse but restored to human form when touched by Rama's feet. Could she have felt more relieved than Hara Bou at this moment?

About to start eating, Baraju paused and said to Hara Bou, "Call Chhakadi!" Hara Bou went to the door of Chhakadi's room and called him, as though she was under a spell. Chhakadi had already raised his hand three times to strike her but Hara Bou seemed determined to forget the past.

Chhakadi said he would attend to a few customers who were waiting at the shop to be served and come back and join Baraju. Hara Bou was deliriously happy; it seemed to her that the world was full of good human beings; everyone was her friend! Netramani hadn't spoken to her but Hara Bou now went to her, took her by the hand warmly and said, "Sana Bohu, come, we will eat a couple of *pithas* together. Chhakadi has gone to the shop; who knows when he will return?"

"The wretched woman is putting on a show to please her husband!" thought Sana Bohu. She would soon put a stop to that! "I am not hungry," the younger *bohu* said. "It's much too early. You go and eat!"

"Sana Bohu," Hara Bou said, "forget the past! I'm your elder sister; if I said something harsh to you at any time, don't keep it knotted up in the end of your sari!"

Hara Bou's words pricked Netramani like needles. She said to herself, "When the husband and the wife weren't on speaking terms, one faced south when the other faced north! And now that there is a little good feeling between them, she has come to try out her tricks on me!"

"Why should anyone say anything to me or why should I say anything to anyone?" the younger *bohu* said to Hara Bou in a flat, sullen tone, and turned away.

Hara Bou did not reply. She returned to Baraju and told him what had happened.

Baraju heard her out and then said, "Very well, until Sana Bohu has eaten, you will not eat either!"

Hara Bou looked at her husband and smiled; he looked at her and smiled back. When had they last looked at each and smiled; neither could remember. Baraju saw his own smile mirrored in Hara Bou's face and she saw her smile reflected in Baraju's.

Baraju realised that since the day they had been married, Hara Bou and he had been partners only in name. The priest had tied their hands together on the marriage *bedi*, but there had always been a wall between them. Today Baraju had boldly pulled down that wall. Hara Bou and he had come together as never before.

Both had discovered each other for the first time and awakened to a new relationship.

Within each human being there is a philosopher's stone which has the power to transform another. Baraju and Hara Bou had transformed each other.

It was past midnight when Chhakadi returned. Neither *bohu* had eaten. Baraju heard the sound of Chhakadi's footsteps at the door and got up. "Where have you been so late in the night?" he asked Chhakadi. Then he called out to Hara Bou. "Chhakadi is here. Get him something to eat." At mealtimes, Baraju always asked Chhakadi to join him, asked him if he had eaten. On some days he was told Chhakadi was away, roaming somewhere, and on other days he was informed that he had already eaten and gone to sleep.

Chhakadi had never been bold enough to stand face to face with his elder brother or to talk back to him. He discussed his affairs only with Netramani, but when he quarrelled it was with his sister-in-law—but only in his brother's absence. Hari Mishra was his only other confidant. No matter how much Netramani tried to goad him, he never had the courage to speak up to his brother. For shame!

Chhakadi retreated into his own room and was talking to Netramani in low tones when Baraju called out again, "Chhakadi, where are you? Food has been served!"

"Yes, I'm coming," Chhakadi said, hurriedly washing his feet and sitting down on the floor, in front of the thali of *pithas*.

Hara Bou went once again to her younger *jaa* and said, "Come, Sana Bohu, let's go and eat! They've all eaten and gone to sleep; there's only you and me left."

"Who asked you to wait for me?" the younger *bohu* said gruffly. She added in a loud aside, "I don't remember her ever waiting for me so we could eat together! Why this show today—as if the rice will lose its taste if we don't eat from the same thali?"

Pretending not to hear, Hara Bou went into her bedroom. Twenty years she had been married, but it was as if she was a new bride once again!

She felt she had no enemies in the world; everyone was a friend. She had lost her youth and her looks but the beauty and youth which she had gained today was not going to fade for five or maybe ten years; it was indestructible.

Hara Bou said to her husband, "Do you hear? When our eldest daughter Hara was married, the sari which we bought for the Sana Bohu was not to her liking. But this time, for Suna's marriage, we must buy her a good sari."

Baraju couldn't believe his own ears. His wife was asking him to buy a good sari for the younger *bohu*!

"Yes, of course," Baraju said. "She will have a good sari. But what about you?" he teased her.

"Am I going to wear a coloured sari at my age?" Hara Bou said. "If my children wear good saris, isn't that enough for me?"

"Are you telling me the truth?"

"Why? Are you the only one who tells the truth?"

"No," Baraju said. "But you are the same person you were earlier, aren't you? Are you sure your mind will always remain the way it is now?"

"Why not? What else could happen?" Hara Bou said, laughing.

"Well, tell me—suppose we lost everything we have and had to go from door to door begging. Would your mind still remain unchanged?"

"Why all this talk? If you became a beggar, would I still be the mistress of a home?

Baraju felt a surge of happiness. The gods had vanquished the demons!

The next morning Hara Bou went to the village pond to bathe. Sharadi Bou and Narayani Pandiyani arrived. The elder bohu was still afloat on a wave of happiness. She felt she had lost her Baraju for a hundred years; now she had found him again. There was not a word of scorn in her mouth for the younger *bohu* or Chhakadi. "What do we have to lose or gain?" she said to her neighbours. "If our children are happily married and settled, our duties are over! Let them build their own homes and enjoy the property. The proverb says, 'If you live in this world, you must learn to put up with falling rocks!' Why should I quarrel? Who should I quarrel with, sister? With my *jaa* and *diara*? Why should I? Who carries anything away when he leaves?"

Sharadi Bou and Narayani Pandiyani stared at her, their mouths open in amazement. Hara Bou went on: "My husband said, 'You can't clap with one hand. Can you say that only those two are at fault and we are blameless? They are mere children—will it help if we take their words to heart?' And isn't it true, sister: am I not to blame? If she did nothing for me, what have I done for her, being the elder? How beautifully he explains everything, sister! 'We cannot see our own faults, but we carry the faults of others in a bundle wherever we go!' It's very true—I've never thought about my own faults! It's no wonder he is praised by people wherever he goes—what a good man he is!"

Hara Bou remained true to the promises she had made to Baraju. She was always attentive to the needs of Chhakadi and his wife. The younger *bohu* thought that this was the care she should have received from her elder *jaa* but had never received. If she was sharing the household work now, she was, in fact, doing more than her share, because it was only her elder *jaa* who had children to be looked after. Three-fourths of the work in this house was because of her. Wouldn't she have done it anyway?

NINE

"Who was it that beat you, Dharamu?" Baraju called out as he walked into Dharamu Bauri's home. Dharamu's back was swollen and blistered where he had been beaten with strands of the poisonous *bichchuati* plant—the stinging nettle. His entire body was bruised black and blue from the blows of thick bamboo sticks. As he entered Dharamu's house, Baraju saw his wife, Dhani Bou, rubbing a little oil into his back. He repeated his question.

Groaning in pain, Dharamu spoke. "Weren't you at home, Baraju Bhai? Give him that wooden plank to sit on," he said to his wife. Then he said to Baraju, "It was young Chandra Sial and Hari Mishra who did it!"

"But why? What happened?"

"You know everything, Baraju Bhai! What could have happened? Mishra had been nursing a grudge for a long time—and he got his chance! I had said something to him at Chhakadi's shop that he didn't like, and from that day he was burning with anger. This morning, my bullock got into his banana patch and that enraged him! He dragged me out of my house and tied me to a coconut tree—what could I say to him, anyway?—but that's the way I always speak!"

A few tears appeared in Baraju's eyes. Alas, poor Dharamu! How many Dharamus had their backs split open? How many

Barajus shed tears over them! Was there anything that anyone could do?

Dharamu said, "He has made me swallow bitter medicine this time but I will show him when *my* time comes! What do I have to lose? People like me have cut away all four ropes—there is nothing to tie us down! If we work in someone's fields, we can get enough to take care of our bellies; do we have property which ghosts can eat up? When I received a tiny homestead plot in my name in this year's *bandobast*, Hari Mishra decided he had to take revenge. 'Just wait!' he told me. 'I'll grow brinjals on your land!' I knew he was out to get me and I told my wife, 'Smash those bangles which you are wearing on your hand! Your husband won't last very long and you will become a widow very soon! But you don't need to worry! You are only a low-caste *bauri* woman! When your husband is dead you can set up home with anyone who takes your fancy! Or if you don't want to do that, you can stay here and work as a labourer in someone's home. You won't have to go hungry.'"

Baraju could not follow what Dharamu was trying to say, "What is all this meaningless babbling, Dharamu?" he said.

"It is not babbling!" Dharamu replied, rolling his eyes. "Here, have a look at this! I've smeared it with some *sindura* and *chua* from Maa Mangala's statue." He pulled out a large *katuri* that he had hidden under the mattress and showed it to Baraju. It had been honed to a sharp edge. "Won't this be enough to slice off a man's neck?"

Baraju Padhan was quivering like a leaf. Instinctively, he moved back a few paces from where he had been sitting. "What's this you are saying, Dharamu?" he said.

"What is there to say now?" Dharamu said. "I'll stand in the middle of the haat tomorrow and shout so loudly that everyone will hear! Either way I am a dead man; why should I fear anyone? Whether I die on the stake, hang from the gallows or die in my sleep—it's all the same! Why should Dharamu be scared?"

Baraju was gripped by fear. Such talk from Dharamu's mouth! He gripped Dharamu's hands and said, "Dharamu, my brother! Control yourself! Be a little patient! Maa Mangala's temple has to be cleansed and purified this evening. I have come to call you. Will you come?"

Dharamu had no interest in temple rituals. He said in the same faraway tone, "Baraju Bhai, the corpse has its head pointing either north or south. Now it is Dharamu Bauri who will perform Hari Mishra's funeral!"

"Dharamu!" Baraju said anxiously. "Listen to me! Come to the temple with me this evening."

"No, Baraju Bhai," Dharamu said. "But don't worry—what has happened to me is nothing! I've had worse beatings."

But that evening Dharamu did present himself at Mangala's temple. Baraju had arrived much earlier. Incense and *jhoona*—powdered resin—were kept burning in earthen braziers inside the temple and the thick, fragrant smoke billowed out into the yard. One by one the other villagers arrived—Jayee Khatai, Bhadei Sutar, Rupa Jena, Jadu Dalei. They came, prostrated themselves before the goddess's image and gathered at the foot of the *malati* creeper outside the temple.

It was Jadu Dalei who spoke first. "Baraju Bhai," he said, "it is all one's *kapala*! Dharamu Das is a poor man, a *bauri*. What harm can he do to anyone? But it was in his *kapala* to receive this beating!"

Baraju said, "Jadu, didn't I tell you the other day—there is no such thing as *kapala*! It is Hari Mishra who makes Dharamu's *kapala*—sometimes good, sometimes ill, depending on Hari Mishra's wish!"

"No brother," said Jadu. "I don't believe that. It isn't Hari Mishra who makes Dharamu's *kapala*—rather, it is Dharamu's *kapala* that makes Hari Mishra!"

"You can say the same thing in different ways, but the meaning will be the same," Baraju said. "'Ramchandra was born as Ravana's evil star' or 'Ravana's evil star was born as Ramchandra'—it is the same. We are ruled by karma, you say; but does that mean we must close our eyes and meditate in silence? How many things don't people do to counter the effects of an evil planet?"

"That is true, Baraju Bhai!"

"Then what can *we* do to ward off this evil planet that has appeared?" Baraju said.

"Baraju Bhai, I have the means to deal with Hari Mishra! Haven't I shown it to you already?" Dharamu shouted from the rear of the group.

Bhadei Sutar, one of the younger members of the group, said, "Today it is Hari Mishra's turn to beat us up, tomorrow it will be the zamindar's *gumashta*, and the next day the mahajan's *piyada*! Have we been born only to be beaten?"

"No, no; not to be beaten only but also to beat!" someone shouted.

"This is foolish talk!" Baraju said. "There are so many families of *chasas* in this village—has anyone among us dared to beat up someone? Not that we don't ever beat up people—we beat up our own people, our own kin! When there's a quarrel among us, we don't know how to settle the dispute and so outsiders have to be called in to intervene."

Uday Sutar said, "What Baraju says is true, brothers! If we didn't quarrel among ourselves, would the *aminas* demand bribes?"

Baraju said, "Dharamu was beaten—but who beat him? If one of us—Chandra Sial—had not helped Hari Mishra, could this have happened? The truth is, we are not united. When Dharamu is beaten his neighbour Udia smiles and says, "What has happened is good!" But if we can feel that when Dharamu is beaten all of us are beaten, if we can share the sorrow when one *domb* house is burnt down or one *bauri* father loses his son, our troubles will disappear like water! Could Hari Mishra have done such wicked things in the midst of so many good men? How many of us witnessed Dharamu being beaten but did nothing?"

Two or three of the men said, "What could we have done? Should we have stood there and allowed ourselves to be beaten?"

"Yes," Baraju said slowly, "that is exactly what we should have done—allowed ourselves be beaten! Weren't we all beaten when Dharamu was beaten? Some among us have been beaten in the past; some will be beaten tomorrow. What do you say then—was it Dharamu alone that was beaten or was it all of us?"

Old Ratana Bhoi said, "All of us. He is right."

Rupa Jena said, "But what could we have done? You know what Hari Mishra is like! Would he have listened to anyone?"

Baraju said, "Ten of you should have stood there forming a ring around Dharamu. You should have said, "*Mishrey Agnya*, Dharamu has committed a mistake today. We could all commit some mistake tomorrow. You are a big man; you take other men out to graze—but we are only poor *mulias* who graze cattle. Please listen to us: if Dharamu has said something wrong or done something wrong, let five men sit together and decide what punishment he should get. But if you have already decided to beat him, then beat all of us!"

Laughing, Rupa said, "Would Hari Mishra have listened to all this? We would have been soundly thrashed—that's all!"

Baraju said, "Yes, and a good thing it would have been! You would have been beaten for Dharamu's sake—for your brother's sake! Would that be such a bad thing? Today Hari Mishra beats Dharamu, tomorrow you, the day after, me! For each one of us that he tries to beat, he will have to beat twenty-five! How many can he beat? People do get beaten! One of two things can happen: either we hide inside our homes like thieves, scared of being beaten, or we stand together with our chests bared, challenging him to beat us. Tell me, which would be the more brave, the more human thing to do?"

Jadu Dalei said, "But has dharma disappeared completely? Will injustice rule the world?"

Rupa said, "It's easy to say these things. There are so many of us here; has anyone agreed to do this?"

Baraju Padhan stood up now and said, "I shall do it! I shall fall at Hari Mishra's feet; and if he doesn't listen, I shall embrace Dharamu, stand there and say, 'Hit me as much as you like; kill me—but I shall never let Dharamu go; he is my brother!' How would it matter if I lost my life? How would it matter if this entire village was emptied of people—if the houses of a hundred poor peasants of Padhanpada were burnt down? Isn't it better for us to be killed than to live like ants and flies? Do you think we are so weak and helpless? Look at the *duba* grass! Goats and sheep graze on it; elephants trample it beneath their feet—but is it destroyed? Then how can we, who have been fortunate enough to be born as human beings, live in fear of a single Hari Mishra?"

Someone shouted, "But is this possible?"

Baraju said, "It is through our own fault that we are killed. If five of us stand together, the Hari Mishras will vanish like smoke! Do not think we are useless, brothers! We are *mulias* who till the soil, who make crops grow out of barren rock!"

Old Ratana Bhoi said, "Our lives are short anyway. How does it matter whether we live or die? The proverb says, 'Don't kill me—I am dead already!' Are we living now that someone can kill us?"

Jadu Dalei said, "No, but perhaps we could begin to live if we did these things!"

"There will be a day when no one will come to help when there is a death in your house and the corpse lies rotting!" said Rupa Jena. "That is what is happening to us!"

Wiping his face with his *gamuchcha*, Baraju said, "Our lives are such that sorrow and pain never leave us! But what do you say, brothers: shall we remain united, in happiness and sorrow, helping each other when there is need? Speak up!"

Each was poking the others: "What do you say? Why don't you speak?"

Jadu Dalei said, "Brothers, there is no need for anyone to hesitate; no one is asking you for money. Whatever we do will be done with our own hands! We are all brothers in the village, all one family! We must stay united; there can be no divisions as there are now. When I am in trouble, you must come and stand at my door and I will come to your help when you need me! Tell me, Rupa Bhai—is this better? Or is it better for me to sharpen my claws each time there is a quarrel in your house?"

"Do you need to ask?" Rupa Jena said. "But what I say is this—will all this happen in a single day? There may be some among us who will want to break away."

Baraju said, "We will do everything necessary to bring them back—hold their hands, fall at their feet! If nothing else works, we will declare them to be *achchuan*—untouchable! Aren't there people in our village now whom no one will touch? Those who refuse to share the sorrows of others, who never do anything to help the village, will be treated the same way!"

Jadu Dalei said, "Yes, that should work! Who would want to be cut off from the others?"

Baraju said, "Very well then, let ten among us volunteer to begin this work. Those who have gone astray have to be brought back to the path! We are human beings, aren't we? What is it that human beings cannot do? We shall make the village a better place; we shall not fear abuse or violence. Not even death! I shall be one among the ten—the first to jump into the fire! Jadu, Nidhia, Rupa,

Udia, Netra, Dharamu, will you join me?"

"Yes!" they shouted together.

"We will do all that can be done," said Jadu. "But remember, Baraju, there is very little in man's hands. It is God who does everything."

"Yes, but what God wants to do, He does through us," Baraju said, smiling. "Is God separate from Man?"

Everyone got up, preparing to go home. As they were walking back, Dharmu came up to Baraju. "You can do what you like, Baraju Bhai," Dharamu said, "but I am not going to give up my *katuri*!"

"You will have to throw that *katuri* of yours into the water before I do anything else," Baraju said.

At a little distance away, Banchcha Rout was saying to Rupa Jena, "Baraju Bhai seems to be well read; he speaks wisely!"

"Don't you know, Baraju Padhan was a government *amina* for five years?"

Rupa said, "Would the government have given him a job if he wasn't educated? But how can you understand these things—you are illiterate yourself!"

TEN

Suna's wedding was to take place in the month of *Ashwin*. There were so many things to be done before the wedding—paddy had to be parboiled and pounded in pestles to remove the husk, *biri* would be ground to a paste on stone slabs and moulded into *badis*. Hara Bou did not have a moment to spare.

But Netramani's mind was made up. "I will go home to my mother!" she told Chhakadi. "Write to my brother and ask him to come and take me home!"

Chhakadi looked up at the sky. Division of the home seemed to be the only way out.

Later that day, Chhakadi was giving instructions to Sania Bhoi, the part-time *mulia* who worked for Baraju Padhan six months in the year and did odd jobs for the remaining six months.

"Sania," Chhakadi said, "this year I am going to have my own *khala* on the five-acre *chaka* and store the *mooga* there after the harvest. I want you to mark off the place on the ground where the *khala* will come up."

Sania stared at Chhakadi in surprise.

"Can't you understand what I'm saying?" Chhakadi said, a little angrily.

"But why do you need another *khala*?" Sania Bhoi said.

"Don't ask questions! Just do what I tell you!" Chhakadi said. "A ginger seller doesn't need to haggle over a ship's price!"

"Ginger seller...ship's price—I don't understand," Sania said. "You want to separate? From a brother like Baraju Padhan? A man who is a lump of gold!"

"Who wants your advice? Do only what you are told to do!"

"All right, all right—I am only a *mulia*; what can I understand of these things?" Sania replied. But to himself he said, "Is this a human being? Can a man like Baraju Padhan have a brother like Chhakadi?"

Baraju was not at home; he had left two days ago to buy a bullock at a cattle fair in a neighbouring village. When he returned home, he heard what had happened. Smiling, he said to Hara Bou, "Well, the boy is learning to take care of his own needs, which is a good thing! What do you say?"

"Yes, it is a good thing," she agreed. "And how does it harm us?" She smiled too. She did not understand these things very well but of one thing she was sure: Baraju would never do anything that was unfair, never say anything that was not the truth. Besides, what difference was there between Baraju and herself?

Chhakadi's new *khala* was ready. Baraju went there the next day. The newly harvested *mooga* had been piled up in the *khala*.

"Sania," Baraju asked, "from which field has this *mooga* come?"

"From the five-acre *chaka*," Sania said.

"Is the rest of the *mooga* dry?"

"Yes, it is ready to be harvested. We are going to pull it out of the fields tomorrow and pile it in your *khala*."

"What do you mean, my *khala*?" Baraju said. "Whose *khala* is this, then?" There was a faint smile on his lips.

"I thought you knew!" Sania said. "This is Chhakadi's new *khala*; he made me scratch it out of the fields. His *mooga* will be stored here—separately from yours."

"What's this talk of his and mine, Sania? If we are going to talk about his and mine, then everything is his; nothing is mine! Bring the remaining *mooga* here after it has been harvested."

"So you are saying all the *mooga* will go to Chhakadi?" Sania asked. He could not believe his own ears.

"Yes!" Baraju said, smiling. "I have been taking it all these years; let him have it now!"

"All of it?" Sania asked again. "It will not be divided?"

"You idiot, have you ever seen anything being divided in this house?" Baraju said. "Whatever was mine was his as well. If the *mooga* goes to Chhakadi, isn't is as good as mine?"

Sania was unable to understand what was happening. He merely did what he was told; he carried the remaining *mooga* over to Chhakadi's *khala* and dumped it there.

"What's this, Sania? "Chhakadi asked him. "Why have you piled all the *mooga* here, in one place?"

"Baraju told me to do it!" Sania was getting irritated.

"Eh, what?"

"Your elder brother! He told me all the *mooga* would go to you."

This was enough to make even a rishi tear out his own hair in frustration! Chhakadi had thought: partition between the brothers would happen easily. But what complication was this?

When Netramani heard what had happened she said, "Well, good! If your brother wants to show the village what a saint he is—let him! You can collect all the *mooga* and sell it in the market."

Hari Mishra said, "It was the cat's good luck that brought the *shika* down! Such a chance is not to be missed!"

Chhakadi said, "No, *Kakei*, I don't like what has happened. My brother will treat every matter the same way and the house will never be partitioned! And then there are the marriages of two daughters and a son to be performed!"

"That's where the real problem lies!" Hari Mishra said, with a wink. "You are a smart bird, Chhakadi! Can anything escape your eyes?"

Chhakadi felt inflated when he was praised by Hari Mishra. "It isn't difficult for me to find out what is happening, although that wife of mine thinks I am a fool."

"Who is clever if you are a fool?" Hari Mishra said.

"Well, now that the matter of the *mooga* is settled, do you know what I am going to do next? " Chhakadi said.

"Take care of the *gooda*?" Hari Mishra said.

"Right you are, *Kakei*! Who can outsmart you? Yes, *Kakei*, we were talking about the *gooda*, weren't we? Out of ten or twelve large slabs of *gooda*, I was given only two for my shop; the rest my brother kept for himself. Three or four pieces were used up by the family while a few were sold. I hear he has saved two pieces for the wedding!"

"Well, I must tell you then! Out of twelve slabs of *gooda*, your share should have been six, right—but you got only two! That means another four pieces are due to you. Now, whether those four pieces were sold or eaten or have been stored in the house makes no difference. They are yours!"

"That's what my wife has been saying! 'Why are those pieces of *gooda* lying in the middle room?' she says. 'They belong to us! Bring them to our room!'"

"I'm not surprised!" Hari Mishra said. "The family she comes from knows how to take care of its belongings. Whatever she says will have some practical wisdom."

That afternoon Chhakadi went to the middle room, picked up the three slabs of *gooda* one by one and carried them to his own room. Hara Bou saw everything but said nothing. Over his shoulder Chhakadi said, "I am taking these for my shop. If you need more *gooda* for the wedding, you can buy it."

When Baraju came home Hara Bou said to him, "What's this? Why did Chhakadi take away all the pieces of *gooda?*"

Smiles never left Baraju's face now, although he looked odd when he smiled, since he had rarely smiled before. He said, "We are going to buy some more for the wedding. That's why he took them."

"But why should we buy *gooda?*" she said.

"Otherwise there will be no wedding!"

Hara Bou decided to ask no more questions. No purpose would be served.

When Sania Bhoi heard what Chhakadi had done, he said, "Can you imagine such a thing? Who was it that kept watch over the fields and drove away the jackals at midnight, who carried water to the fields, who looked after the sugarcane—and look who is going to eat the *gooda* now!"

Netra Ojha said, "Could such a thing have happened in earlier days? Does anyone separate from such a brother? He is just doing what others teach him; he has no brains of his own!"

"Only someone without brains would do what he is doing," Sania said. "Look at Baraju; is there another man like him in the village? Have you ever seen him sitting idle? Whatever he earns is spent on the family. Where did the money for Chhakadi's shop come from? Did Baraju ever want a paisa back? Two pieces of *gooda* had been saved for the wedding and even that you took away, Chhakadi! What a small mind you have!"

Baraju had only one wish now: there should be no whiff outside of what was happening within the home! The family was already in danger of splitting up because of outside interference but Baraju was not aware of it. Who could break up his family unless he himself wanted it? How could the two brothers in his own house be separated when he was trying to make a single family out of the entire village? He had promised his father: no dividing wall would come up in the middle of the house. Would Baraju Padhan break his word?

A tender branch might break, but it would not bend. Baraju Padhan was a true son of his father. The marriage of his eldest daughter, Hara, had passed off smoothly; so would the marriages of Suna and Moti—he was confident of that. Had he gone into debt over Hara's wedding? Or had he dug up some hidden treasure to perform the wedding? Whatever he earned through his own labour had sufficed. Why should he have any fears for Suna and Moti? He who had given birth to them, He who filled the mother's breasts with milk even before the child was born—would He not take care of everything? Why should Baraju worry?

> Everything I do, everything I get done
> Without my wish this world cannot run.

Suna's wedding was performed. An expensive sari was purchased for the younger *bohu*, but she was not to be satisfied. "Perform one marriage after another!" she grumbled. "You have already emptied the house! And now you get a sari for me, just to please me. Keep your sari; I don't want it!"

Through how many ages had the stream of human existence flowed uninterrupted? One generation fell and the next trampled it underfoot, oblivious to the cries of pain. Each one was swept ahead in the current, unable to stand still. Wave followed wave; some drowned while others were carried away; no one thought of another. No one hesitated to drink the blood of his own brother, his own kin. When would man become civilised? Forests had given way to elegant habitations but human nature had remained what it was—full of envy, hatred and pride. The earth went round and round the sun, creating night and day, months and seasons—

but the steady onward flow of the human race was unchanged. Wars were fought; kings and emperors rose and disappeared. Ages passed: the *Satya Yuga*, the *Dwapara Yuga* and then the *Kali Yuga*. Who had been able to keep his place in the face of this unceasing flow? Baraju Padhan? What did he count for? He was merely a piece of straw floating away on the tide. He had suddenly come to a halt while struggling against whirlpools, patches of foam, bubbles…Wait, wait—who was that calling out to me? It sounded like a human voice. Alas for the human race! Weren't the earth, the sea and the sky big enough for you—then what was this that you were doing? It was your own brother, your own race that you were treading upon! Someone was burning with fever; someone was starving; here was a mother with dry breasts, unable to feed her baby. This man's back had been scarred by lashes but there was no one to soothe his wounds.

Oh mankind! Pause for a moment! How many generations had gone; how many kings and emperors had passed—pause awhile! Why don't you listen to the voice that is calling—it's a human voice, isn't it?

Baraju Padhan had come to a halt while the tide flowed on. He had heard the cries of pain and hunger. Why should he fear anyone? Even death? What life was he living, anyway? Who needed him? Who would weep for him if he should die? Thousands were dying everyday, of disease, of hunger. Beaten like cattle by Hari Mishras, with no one to listen if they should weep or howl. Dying unseen, unknown. Baraju Padhan would be one of them; he would die a similar death. "Oh dharma! It is you that holds the world together! Kings and beggars are alike to you! To those that have wealth, power, bring some compassion! How many Dharamu Bauris are there in the world, condemned to be beaten from the day they are born to the day of their death! They are no longer human; they are living ghosts! Oh dharma! Teach them how to live in dignity like human beings. Let the great look upon the miserable with pity, with love! Let there be an end to hatred and strife!" Baraju's eyes grew moist.

Just then: "Baraju Bhai! Baraju Bhai!"

He got up hurriedly. "Nita! What brings you here at this hour?"

Nitei Moharana was bathed in dust from head to foot. As soon as he saw Baraju, he burst into tears like a child. "Baraju Bhai, I am finished!" he howled. "My children are going to starve! Where can I find fifty rupees?"

"What happened?"

Nita covered his head with both hands in despair. "My daughter was married two months ago and I had to borrow ten rupees to feed my caste brothers," he said. "I have already paid back twenty rupees to clear the loan and the interest but when I asked for the paper to be returned I was told the amount I must pay is fifty rupees! 'I am a poor man; where can I find so much money?' I said to him, whereupon he said, 'Why? All of you sat together in the village and decided to unite against me, didn't you? Which one of your fathers will come and pay up your loan now?' Who will help me now, Baraju Bhai?"

"Who gave you the loan, Nitei? Baraju asked. "Was it Hari Mishra? Why didn't you tell him how much money you had already repaid and on which dates?"

"What more could I have said, Baraju Bhai? I cried, rolled in the dust before him, but nothing was of any use. 'Go, go!' he said. 'Ask your leader to come and pay.'

"Calm yourself, Nitei," Baraju said. "Be patient! Do you think such injustice can prevail?"

"Baraju Bhai, I have no hopes! I am sunk! But maybe He who sits above, He who creates day and night, will judge!"

Baraju's eyes filled with tears. His voice quivered as he said, "Yes, He will judge, Nitei—He will judge!"

Was there anything that a man could do? Was there anything that Baraju could do? But He who had created Baraju as well as Hari Mishra, He who observed everything—surely He would set things right. And it would be through a human being such as Baraju that His wish would find expression.

ELEVEN

Suna's wedding was over. Netramani did not wear the sari that was bought for her. Baraju Padhan bought *mooga* and *gooda* for his daughter's wedding. Chhakadi sold *mooga*, sold *gooda*. The goldsmith made a necklace for Netramani.

Chhakadi said to Hari Mishra, "*Kakei*, my brother does not say a word to anything I do. I sold the *mooga*, sold the *gooda*, spent the money on my wife's necklace, but neither he nor my *bhauja* said a word. But that wife of mine insists we must have our own kitchen. 'They have a handful of children,' she says. 'There's still Moti to be married. Gifts will be sent every month to the married daughters and their in-laws.The son needs a bowl of milk every morning. What else can your brother and *bhauja* do but keep their mouths shut? It is to their own advantage!' But *Kakei*, my mind is uneasy. I wish my brother would say something! Earlier, my *bhauja* used to quarrel over everything but now even she is surprisingly quiet. Now tell me, *Kakei*, how long can I keep up this one-sided fight? What will people in the village say? But my wife says, 'Let them speak ill of us. How does it matter? Are they going to fill up my house with things?'"

Hari Mishra said, "What did I tell you, Chhakadi? Children will always take after their parents! Your wife comes from prosperous home; what do you expect? You are a fool! There are all kinds of people in the village; they will say all kinds of things! Why listen to them? Does everyone in the village speak well of me? But is that a reason why I should fear them? Let them bark!"

"Yes, I understand all that, *Kakei*," Chhakadi said. "But still, I feel uncomfortable. How can I demand a separate kitchen when my brother says 'yes' to everything?"

"You don't understand, Chhakadi! A separate kitchen is not the answer—that's only woman's talk! You may eat separately for a couple of days if your kitchens are separated, but then you'll come together again, separate again! Do you want this to go on? One day you will have to break away like the man you are! Everything will have to be divided—fields, cattle, utensils, everything! What use is it if you are out today and back again the next day?"

"*Kakei*, I don't understand what I should do," Chhakadi said. "She says, 'We'll start with separate kitchens, then go on to divide the fields and cattle and everything else. Let them add up the expenses on the marriages of the two daughters and give us half."

"You are lucky, Chhakadi; how many people get such a wife? She's always giving you the right advice—and still you say you feel uncomfortable! What problems are there for you now, Chhakadi? All you have to do is to find three respectable men in the village to act as mediators, make a list of everything in the house and divide it up equally. What is so difficult about that?"

"What you say is quite right, *Kakei*," Chhakadi said. "But I can't go looking for three mediators in the village. It will be enough if you are there to mediate. But there's one thing—I have never spoken to my brother about partition. How am I going to bring up this matter now?"

"You fool!" Hari Mishra said, irritated. "Who is going to teach you these things? If you cannot open your mouth in your brother's presence, how are you going to become independent? Go then, stay where you are!"

Chhakadi said, "But that wife of mine won't leave me in peace! No, *Kakei*, you will have to come over to the house tomorrow morning! Nothing will happen unless you are there!"

"*Arre dhat*!" Hari Mishra said. "How do I make you understand? What good will my going there do if you will not say anything at all to your brother?"

"No, *Kakei*, I'll raise the matter today at home."

But the matter wasn't raised that day. That evening Chhakadi saw his brother Baraju squatting on the verandah outside, writing on a piece of dried palm leaf with an iron stylus. He was making a copy of the tenth chapter of the *Bhagabata*. His father, old Shaama Padhan, had copied the first four chapters and had asked Baraju to copy out the rest. There was a scratching sound as Baraju inscribed the letters carefully on the dry palm leaf. He was totally absorbed in the task.

How could Chhakadi talk to him now about the partition of the house? He went back to his own room. He said to Netramani, "Bhai is alone on the verandah. This looks like a good time to speak to him about partition. Shall I speak to him?"

"Yes, why don't you?" she said. "Do you have to ask me everything?"

Chhakadi went back to the verandah. Baraju was still writing. He had not noticed Chhakadi's presence. Chhakadi shuffled around for a few minutes and returned to his room once again. Netramani looked up.

"What should I say to him?" Chhakadi said.

She glared at him angrily. "Say whatever you like," she said, "but don't come back to me. I am tired of your *maichia* ways!"

Such an insult from his own wife! *Chhi*, *chhi*! He would speak out—no matter what happened.

Stepping into the verandah, Chhakadi called out, "Bhai!"

Baraju stopped writing, looked up and saw Chhakadi. "Did you call me?" he asked.

The words Chhakadi had planned to speak dried up in his throat. "No, no!" he said hurriedly. "I was going out!"

Baraju went back to his writing.

Chhakadi had fetched the *mooga* and *gooda* but on neither occasion had he been required to confront Baraju directly. How could he speak to him now about partition? It was easy for others to call him names—but let them come out and speak if they dared!

The next morning, Baraju awoke while it was still dark and went out to water his fields, which were getting parched for want of rain. Sania Bhoi was with him. Other farmers were watering their fields, close to him as well as in the distance, and the sounds of their conversation and singing mingled with the splash of water being transported to the fields in buckets. The stars were reflected in the water. The trees and houses in nearby villages were faint shadows as they peeped out of the darkness and gradually became more distinct. The east turned pink and then crimson as light spread across the sky. A flock of cranes, appearing to be dressed in white clothes, could be seen searching for insects in the rice fields. Crows, sparrows and kites filled the sky with their screeching. The villages in the distance were draped in mist, as though wearing a white shawl.

Having watered his fields, Baraju Padhan turned around to return home, carrying on his head a bundle of grass which had been mown the night before. The tender rice plants growing in the small patch of land were moist with dew. When he reached his house, Baraju saw Hari Mishra and Chhakadi chatting together on the verandah.

On seeing Baraju, Hari Mishra said, "Out so early in the morning, Baraju? Don't you get any sleep at night? Well—you are always so careful; you get no peace unless you do everything yourself!"

Baraju put down the grass at the entrance to his cattle shed and sat down on the verandah. "*Juhaar, Kakei*!" Baraju said. "What brings you here so early?"

"This brother of yours gives me no rest!" Hari Mishra said. "'Come at once, *Kakei*! We brothers are going to be separated; the house will be partitioned! If you don't come, no one will know what to do!' *Arre*, I have other things to do; how can I get entangled in this business?"

"Who is going to be separated, *Kakei*? What is all this about—I don't understand!" Baraju said.

Pretending to be surprised, Hari Mishra said, "*Eyn*! What's this? You don't know? Then was the boy lying to me? Oh, this is too much! He has been pestering me for the last three months. '*Kakei*, come! Our house has to be partitioned! You will have to draw the lots to decide who gets what,' I told him. 'Why are you thinking of partition? You are just a child!' But he wouldn't listen. 'No, *Kakei*!' he said. 'There is no other way. The family expenses are mounting—there are still two nieces and a nephew to be married. How much property do we own, anyway? I cannot afford these expenses! Let my brother give me my half of the property and also give me an account of the money he spent on the two weddings; after that, we will go separate ways! Why should I get my feet muddy and have to wash them again and again?' I have had no rest at all this past month! Everyone wants me to come and look after his affairs while my own fields are drying up!"

What Hari Mishra did not say was that meddling in the affairs of others was his principal business—and a highly profitable one at that!

Baraju laughed and said, "Did Chhakadi drag you here so early in the morning just for this small matter? Brothers will be separated, the house will be partitioned—is that such a serious matter that you have to be brought here when you have so many more important things to do? *Kakei*, go home, I beg you! This Chhakadi is an irresponsible lad—you know my mother called him 'Chagala', don't you? Pay no attention to what he says!"

"Say no more, son!" Hari Mishra said. "I tried my best to make him understand, but would he listen? 'No, *Kakei,*' he said. 'You have got to help me! You are like my own father!'"

"Who can deny that?" Baraju said. "But does that mean you must give up all other work and run here?"

Hari Mishra stood up and wiped both feet with his *gamuchcha.* "Oh very well, if he called me, he called me! It is no great crime that he has committed! But what I was saying was—Chhakadi, where are you? Look at the boy—how can he run away when such an important matter is being discussed?"

Chhakadi had, in fact, made good his escape the moment he saw his brother approaching. Hari Mishra returned home fuming at Chhakadi's behavior. He had been exposed unnecessarily.

Baraju realised that Chhakadi was bent upon splitting up the home. "Let me see how anyone can break up this home while Baraju Padhan is alive!" he said to himself. He called Chhakadi and said with a smile, "Chhakadi, what need is there to call in mediators if you want to separate? The property is ours; it is we who will decide how it is to be divided—what can outsiders do? But tell me first, why are you so keen on partition?"

Netramani had spent months tutoring her husband; Hari Mishra had given him innumerable lessons. Would all this go in vain? Chhakadi said, "Why should I not be keen? Whatever income we have is spent entirely on meeting your needs: two marriages were performed, so many people have to be fed! I can no longer manage this confusion!"

Baraju was amazed—such words from Chhakadi's mouth! The same Chhakadi who had never dared to raise his head and speak up to his brother? No, no, this could not be Chhakadi; it was somebody else in Chhakadi's form!

Baraju said, "Chhakadi, you are determined to have a partition of the house and I am equally determined that there shall be no division of this house, the fields, the cattle! Then tell me how your desire as well as mine can be fulfilled? Can you think of a way?"

What was Baraju trying to say? Chhakadi was unable to understand. He said, "I cannot find an answer to these riddles. The simplest thing will be to divide everything into two halves. Why these puzzles?"

Baraju said strongly, "I have just told you there will be no division. Everything will remain whole and undivided."

"And I have told you that I cannot live in this house together with you!" Chhakadi said just as strongly.

"I haven't said no to that!" Baraju said. "We shall separate, but the property will remain undivided. Then both of us will have our desires fulfilled."

"I cannot understand when things are said in such a roundabout way," Chhakadi said. "Just give me an account of all the expenses, including the expenses on Hara's and Suna's marriage, and let everything be divided into two halves." He found it difficult to talk to Baraju about the marriages and seemed to have a bout of coughing.

Baraju said, "No, brother—does anyone talk about the expenses on a daughter's wedding? Should we brothers be discussing this? Have we fallen so low? I am telling you—the property will not be divided. We will separate, but there will be no dividing wall in this house, no hedge across the fields. This house is yours—the fields, orchards, the crops, the trees, the cattle—they are all yours! What do I need them for, tell me? There's only Moti to be married now, and after she is married, I'll be free. I am not worried about my son Dama; he can find work somewhere. And as for the two of us, we will manage! "

Chhakadi was stupefied by Baraju's words. What was he saying? He swallowed his saliva repeatedly and kept staring at this brother, who had suddenly become a stranger to him.

"What is this you are saying?" the words escaped his lips.

"Don't you understand?" Baraju said. "The property will not be divided but we shall live separately. Everything will be yours. I shall leave the house tomorrow with my wife and children. Now do you understand?" He smiled.

Chhakadi was silent for a long time. Then he said one word. "No!"

The 'no' came from his guts, not his lips. It carried no trace of Netramani's stubbornness or Hari Mishra's cunning; it was a simple, straightforward 'no'.

Baraju got up and walked into the house. Hara Bou was standing close to the door. "The other day you were making tall promises, weren't you?" he said to her. "Well, the day has come! We shall have to leave this house after we have handed everything over to Chhakadi. Will you be able to do it?"

At first Hara Bou could not believe what he was saying. "You are lying!" she said.

"Why should I lie to you?' he said. "Have you ever found me lying?"

Then she found his words shocking and not at all to her liking. "How can we leave the house just like that?" she asked. "Where shall we live?"

Baraju laughed. "Where shall we live? Does anyone decide that in advance?"

"But what is this—everything is uncertain, unknown, and you want us to leave the house, as if there are ghosts pursuing us! I've never heard of such a thing!"

"We are leaving tomorrow, Hara Bou," Baraju said quietly. "Early tomorrow morning. If you want to come with me, start preparing!"

What choice was she being offered? "Very well, then," she said. "Just tell me what things to take with us and I'll tie them up in a bundle."

"Not one little kitten nor one cowrie!" he said. "Just a few old clothes, so we can manage!"

"And the utensils?"

"Nothing! And another thing—not a word to anyone!"

"As if I'll lose my taste for food if I don't talk!" Hara Bou said, rebuffed and sulking.

Chhakadi went to his wife, too, and told her everything.

"They don't mean it! They are just trying to give us a scare!" Netramani said. "Who ever heard of anyone giving up his home willingly, and where have these new *mahatmas* come from? All that this family knows how to do is to eat up others' property! Let them go!"

Now she turned her fury upon Chhakadi. "You *maichia*!" she shouted. "Why did you hide your face and run away like a thief? Why didn't you tell them, 'Will you really go? Then why don't you go now?' Who is afraid of these threats? And instead of talking to them like a man, you ran away! *Maichia*—it's you that is responsible for everything."

"Why do you talk like that?" Chhakadi said. "Wait! They are supposed to go tomorrow morning. We will just keep quiet and let things happen."

"Yes, that's the thing to do!" Netramani said.

Her words were echoing in Baraju's ears in the other room. "If you really want to go, then go now!"

TWELVE

The next morning Baraju awoke very early, woke Chhakadi up, called him and showed him everything—the house, the fields, cattle; where the *kolatha* was kept, the paddy seeds—and explained everything. How much property did they own, anyway? It took no more than an hour.

Baraju said, "Now that you have understood everything, shall we separate?"

Chhakadi said, "Yes, if we divide up everything half and half..."

"No, Chhakadi," Baraju said. "I don't want a share at all. Father told us not to divide anything. There will be no division!"

"Very well, do what you like!" Chhakadi said, annoyed. "What can anyone say?"

Baraju went into the house and saw that Hara Bou had put together quite a collection of things—pots and vessels, tin boxes full of clothes and what not. "What's all this?" he said.

"These are what I'm going to take with me," she said.

"Who asked you to take all these things?" he said. "Didn't I say we will take nothing from this house?"

"I had bought all these things and kept them for our use," she said.

"Well, put them away! And if you are taking any clothes or other things with you, show them to the younger *bohu* first!"

Hara Bou looked at him witha question in her eyes. But when Baraju smiled at her, she smiled back. No words were spoken, but each communicated something to the other.

Hara Bou had not said a word to anyone in the village, but within minutes everyone knew—Baraju was leaving home! Sharadi Bou, Nandi Pandiyani, Netra Ma, Shobha Nani, and many other women crowded into the Padhan home. They had brought gifts for Hara Bou: someone was holding a *danta kathi*, someone a lump of *haladi* paste or a small brass *gina* of oil, a piece of dried tobacco rolled into a *pika*.

"*Chhi*! Who ever heard of such a thing? Running away from your own home because your *jaa* picked up a quarrel! Like eating your meals out of a *khapara*, a clay tile, because you are unhappy with the thief who stole your utensils! Couldn't you have divided up the property? If two brothers don't get along, they can set up separate homes. Doesn't this happen in every family?"

Outside the front door a group of men had congregated—Jadu, Nidhia, Maaga, Dharamu, Maguni and others. Wiping his eyes with his *gamuchcha*, Nidhia said, "Baraju Bhai will do what he thinks right—he won't listen to anyone! Who can make him change? He is like the *rukuna ratha*—the chariot that never returns!"

Dharamu said, "Does Baraju Bhai think he can leave us and go away? It won't be that easy!"

Jadu laughed and said, "What will you do to stop him, Dharamu?"

"What will I do?" Dharamu said. "I'll follow him wherever he goes! If he can give up so much property, why can't I give up my huge zamindaris?"

Maaga said, "You know, what Dharamu says isn't entirely wrong! If Baraju goes away from this village, there will be no meaning in our remaining here. Old Shaama Padhan is dead and now Baraju Bhai is leaving! Why should we remain here?"

Dharamu said, "Well, he may say he will leave but does that mean he has left? How can he go when there are so many of us to stop him? Shall we sit here quietly and watch him go?"

Jadu said sarcastically, "And what great things will you do, Dharamu?"

Dharamu said, "You want to see what I can do? The three of you just sit here and watch! If I don't get Baraju his half share of the property within moments, my name isn't Dharamu Das! Do you think Chhakadi can have his way just because Baraju made one unwise promise? *Huh*! You are dealing with Dharamu Das—nobody else!"

Nidhia said, "Stop talking big, Dharamu! Baraju has already said he wants nothing from this home. Can you drag him into a partition?"

The discussion was swiftly turning into one of the quarrels that were routine in the village. Jadu said, "Keep quiet, all of you! Let us not get into a useless fight."

Baraju saw that his personal affairs were becoming public. But no matter what happened, he would have to go. When Chhakadi told him he wanted to separate, and more so when he brought up the question of Hara and Suna's marriages and demanded an account of the expenses, Baraju was reminded of many past incidents. He remembered what had happened over the *mooga* and the *gooda*. No—not any more! His attachment to the family home did put chains on his feet from time to time, but he realised now that Chhakadi had started planning the division long ago. He remembered the younger *bohu*'s words: "If you want to go, go at once!" No, there was no question of his staying back!

He went in and said to Hara Bou, "Let us go!"

The women of the village were tormenting Hara Bou with a hundred questions: Where will you go? You are a housewife; can you go roaming from village to village? Who has ever heard of such a thing? Why didn't you stop Baraju?

Hara Bou replied, "Would he have listened if I tried to stop him?"

Shobha Nani said, "Hara Bou, you forget you are from a *chasa* home, not a family of *bauris* or *kandras*! How can you go wandering like that?"

But Sharadi Bou said to the others, "What old-fashioned talk is this? Aren't *bohus* from respectable homes going out? Why shouldn't Hara Bou go out?"

"Come, let us not delay!" Baraju said to Hara Bou as he wound the *theka* tightly around his head, picked up the bundle of old clothes and tucked it beneath one armpit. In one hand he held a three-*haath* long stick. As he walked out through the front door he was followed by Hara Bou, holding her infant son in one arm and Moti's hand in hers. She took leave of the other women amid tears and smiles. Various things lay scattered around the house—pots and pans, metal trunks, her patch of *saaga*, the little plant on which green chilies were beginning to appear—but she did not glance at anything. No attachment held her back.

Maaga, Netra, Nidhia, Dharamu and others had resolved that together they would make Baraju give up his plans and return home. But Jadu said, "It will be of no use; no one can do it—not Brahma, Bishnu or Maheswar. You don't know him—he may break but he won't bend! Pray to God that he will be successful in the work that he has taken in hand, that's all—but don't try to do that which cannot be done."

Nidhia said, "If only there was one place where he could find shelter!"

"Baraju Bhai has his home everywhere; why worry about him?" Jadu said. "What is impossible for someone who can walk away from his own home without a thought? Has he any cares—even for his food?"

Baraju walked out of his home smiling, with his stick in his hand. Behind him came Hara Bou, holding Moti's hand, with her youngest son, Dama, clinging to her bosom. She looked back occasionally, smiling and nodding to the village women. Baraju looked at Jadu and said, "Jadu Bhai, now it is you who must look after this village."

"Will I be able to do it alone?" he said.

"Why do you keep repeating the same thing? Are you alone? Am I alone?"

And Jadu remembered the words from the *Bhagabata*:

It is I who do everything
And get everything done!

To Dharamu, Nidhia, Maaga and Netra, Baraju said, "Do not worry, my brothers! There is always someone looking after you. And wherever I may be, I shall always be thinking of you, inquiring about your welfare."

When the others looked at Baraju, their minds were filled with a deep sense of reverence. They had planned to say so many things to him, but words failed them now. They followed him like a flock of sheep.

As Baraju made his way down the village, between the two rows of thatched huts, several elderly and aged men came out of their homes. One frail old man, his hands and legs reduced by fever to mere sticks, said, "Baraju is going? Then dharma is departing from this village!" Baraju bade farewell to each man with a *dandabat*, bowing deeply from the waist with hands joined together. There was not a trace of sorrow or regret on his face.

At the village limit, Baraju turned around and asked the crowd of people that had been following him to return to their homes. Many of them had been busy working in their fields but had dropped everything to come out and watch Baraju leave the village. They stood there with folded hands; some prostrated themselves on the ground. There were no dry eyes in that silent crowd; many were sniffing, trying to hold back their emotions. Baraju spoke to each one, stroking someone's back, doing a *juhaar* to someone, giving someone his blessings.

Baraju walked with long strides, holding his stick in one hand; Hara Bou followed with her two children. "Look, if you walk at that pace how can Moti keep up?" she complained.

"Why don't you say it is you that cannot walk—why are you using Moti as an excuse?" Baraju said, smiling. "But did you take leave of the younger *bohu* when you came away I looked for Chhakadi but didn't see him anywhere."

"Yes, I did tell her I was going," Hara Bou said, "but she just turned around and looked the other way. What could I have done?"

Just then Baraju heard some sounds behind him: someone was running hard, trying to catch up. He stopped and turned around. "*Arre*, Goura? What are you doing here?" he said.

It was Gouranga Sena of Haripur village, a man very close to Baraju. He did not have a moment's peace if he was away from his 'Baraju Bhai'; there were ten occasions each day when he came running to him. Baraju was called on every occasion, happy or sad; he was needed each time there was a quarrel or dispute. Goura would bring some brinjals or cucumbers from his fields and chat away with Baraju for hours. On some days he would eat with Baraju.

Goura came up to Baraju, panting. "Baraju Bhai," he said, unable to speak clearly, "I have just come from your house." His eyes looked red and swollen.

"What is it, Goura?" Baraju said.

"Baraju Bhai, there is one request I have to make to you. Promise me that you will keep my request!"

"What request?" Baraju said. "What is the matter?"

"I'll tell you if you promise!" Goura said.

"How can I promise unless I know what it is?"

"No, first promise that you will keep my request!" Goura knew Baraju's nature. He would never do anything without first thinking about it carefully. If you wanted something out of him you had to approach him cleverly. But once he had given you his word, you could rest easy!

"Baraju Bhai, promise me you will do as I ask!" Goura said, as insistent as a child.

"But how can I promise before you tell me what it is!" Baraju said. "Am I Raja Harishchandra that I can fulfill every promise? All right, you win! Now tell me what it is that you want."

"Baraju Bhai! Come with me!" Gora said, smiling happily. "You will have to spend four days in our home in Haripur. Just four days—not an hour longer. Then you can go wherever you want to go!"

"Listen to me, Goura..." Baraju began.

"I will not listen to anything you say!" Goura said. "You have given me your word; it is up to you know—you can keep your promise or break it!" He began to weep like a child.

Baraju saw there was no other way. "Come," he said to Hara Bou. "He won't let us go! This is the way to his village; let us go!"

That morning, after he had spoken to Baraju and understood all the details of the property, Chhakadi went to the haat in Nagpur. "Will Brother really give up the property and walk away?" he was thinking to himself. Both Netramani and Hari Mishra had warned him—no one did such a thing willingly. Which brother would give up his home to another brother? Then Chhakadi thought—yes, there were examples. Didn't Ramchandra give up the kingdom to Bharat and walk away into the forest? But then, that had happened in another age. Can you expect such a thing to happen today? Nowadays one brother will slit another's throat.

Why, only the other day a brother in a wealthy zamindar family had conspired with the others and got the eldest brother killed, along with his wife and children. For just a small slice of the property! Netramani was right! No brother would do it today. All this was mere bluff!

But then his brother was peculiar; Chhakadi hadn't been able to fathom him till today. At times he appeared to be half mad! God knew what he would do.

At the haat, Chhakadi had no interest in buying anything. All he could think of was what was happening at home.

Then Uchchaba Bhoi came and informed him—his brother had left the home along with his wife and two children.

At first Chhakadi was amazed. Had his brother really left? How strange! Would he never come back? How could *Bhauja* have gone? And Moti and Dama?

"Who went with them?" Chhakadi asked. "Did someone accompany them, carrying things from the house?

"Eh, how is such a thing possible? The husband walks ahead and the wife follows with her children. And they are smiling away! Have they no shame? Have they forgotten which family they are from? Who ever heard of such a thing!"

"But which way did they go? Were they walking towards Cuttack?"

Should he go and call them back? So many people seemed to have tried, but nothing worked.

"Does anyone do such a thing? Throw everything away?"

"Well, you can see for yourself what is happening! What can you expect of someone who makes a stranger of his own brother?"

"He may have walked out on us, but he will surely come back!"

Uchchaba was about to return to Padhanpur after he had finished his business in the haat. Chhakadi called him and asked, "Uchchaba, what was Brother saying when he left?"

Uchchaba became irritated. "Do you think I have nothing else to do that I should be thinking only of such things?" he said.

"Wait, Uchchaba, wait," Chhakadi said, growing soft. "Tell me—was Brother saying anything about me at all?"

"I have no time to talk," Uchchaba said. "I still have many things to do in the haat." He started to walk away.

"Uchchaba, tell me, tell me! *To pua raan*—for your son's sake!" Chhakadi ran after him.

Uchchaba turned around. "What kind of a man are you?" he said. "Didn't I tell you—I didn't hear anything! *Pua raan*, *bapa raan*! What nonsense!"

Chakkadri returned home disappointed. Many people talked to him on the way; many were the questions asked. He remembered Hari Mishra's words: "These small people will talk; just let them! No one is going to help you!"

Chhakadi reached the front door of their house. The whole house was unusually silent. Moti and Dama were not playing outside in the dust today. Baraju was not sitting on the front verandah, copying out the *Bhagabata* or weaving a rope out of strands of jute. Chhakadi entered the house. Not a sound. The stillness was oppressive.

Netramani was busy tidying up the house. Now she was its undisputed mistress, with no one to order her around! There was no *dedhsura* that she had to hide away from; no elder *jaa* to quarrel with her. She could do what she liked. The house was hers.

She saw Chhakadi and came out smiling. "So you have remembered your wife and your home at last!" she said. "Here I am, alone, with no one to help! How much can I do by myself? There are so many things lying around the house."

Netraman's words, for some reason, were not pleasing to Chhakadi's ears today. He thought to himself, "This is all your doing! Who will tidy up the house if you don't?" But to his wife he said, "So has everyone gone? Won't they return?"

"Why don't you go and call them back?" Netramani taunted him, still busy with the pots, pans and baskets.

Chakkadi ate and went out and sat on the front verandah. The house felt so strange, so unfamiliar! "Brother will come back," he thought. "How can he not? Where can he go? And there are *bhauja* and Moti and Dama with him! How long can they wander?"

He came to his room inside the house, then went back to the verandah again. No, nothing was the same! His brother would come back; he had to!

Netramani said, "Why are you walking around restlessly? Why don't you go to their room and see what is lying there? Your brother has dumped everything—you will have to tidy up!"

"Why do you keep croaking like a frog!" he said. "Who is going to run away with his things? The room is bolted."

"Oh *ma*!" Netramani said. "Why are you showing me your temper? If you are so unhappy because your brother has left, why didn't you run after him and call him back?"

"But why are you in such a hurry to examine his things? Can't you wait?"

"What has he left behind? A few pots and baskets? Did he show you what things he was taking?"

Chhakadi suddenly felt very depressed. "He showed me everything—the bundle of old clothes, the *batuas*, everything! There was not a paisa there! How could he have taken anything away?"

"Do you think he would have poked his finger into your eye and said, 'Look, this is what I am taking away! And this is how I will do it!' Be patient! In just four days from now you will be told—your *bhai* and *bhauja* have set up their new home somewhere. Just wait."

And Chhakadi waited patiently. One day, two days, three...But there was no news of his brother. Then Jaga Sethi told him—Baraju was staying in the house of Gouranga Sena of Haripur village! "Is that where he plans to live?" Chhakadi asked. No, no, how long could he stay there?

Three days passed and each day in that house seemed more oppressive. There was no peace for Chhakadi—neither inside the house nor outside it. Why did his brother have to run away as though spirits were after him? If he had told Chhakadi he didn't want to be separated, wouldn't Chhakadi have agreed? (He conveniently forgot the part he had played in the drama!)

It was a hot summer's afternoon. Chhakadi had his meal and lay down to rest in the inner courtyard, just outside his brother's room. He hadn't opened the door to the room at all, but now he suddenly felt a desire to peep inside and see what was in it.

On a mango tree in the backyard sat a *kapota*, sounding its call: "The basket of rice is full; get up, my son; *arise*, *arise*, *arise*!" A raven perched on the roof called out restlessly—*kaw*, *kaw*, *kaw*. Chhakadi's mind grew sad. What a happy home this had been—and what was it now! Whose was the property? Of what use was it? Chhakadi could not understand anything. His mind turned bitter.

He opened his brother's room. Everything was just as it had been. The tin trunk could have been broken open and its contents scattered; the mattress could have been chewed up by rats; the entire room could have been stripped. Then Chhakadi might have felt a little better. His brother hadn't taken a single thing away—everything was just as before. Chhakadi searched every corner—as though he had lost something, as though he could find it somewhere in the dust. His eyes fell on something—it was a child's toy, a rubber duck, which squeaked when it was squeezed. Chhakadi picked it up and hugged it to his chest and his tears flowed in a stream. The family that had left was alleged to have eaten up the entire property—who would eat it now? He took the toy in his hand and looked at it again. It seemed to him as though four pairs of little hands, belonging to four children, were reaching out to hold the toy. He was blinded by his own tears.

Chhakadi looked at Netramani but did not smile or say a word. The earthen floor grew moist with tears where he sat. Netramani looked at him and laughed within herself. "*Maichia*!" she said to herself. "Trying to impress me with his tears! That's how he will behave for a day or two and then he will be his usual self again!"

Chhakadi did not go to his shop that evening. He sat on the verandah, all hunched up. On the road outside, old Sadhua Ma staggered along holding her stick, struggling to cover up her body with the torn rag she was wearing. She was very old and her eyesight was failing. "So this is what had to happen at last!" she muttered to herself. "This was in your mind! Did he ever harm anyone? He wouldn't even hurt a fly! Is there another like him in the village? Would this have happened if old Shaama Padhan was still living?"

Chhkadi got up quickly and rushed into the house. "Bhai! Bhai!" he called out. What was happening to him? Would he go mad? He was unable to eat one handful of rice without his tears mingling with it; at night, he blabbered in his sleep, "Bhai!"

Netramani spoke to him, and asked him many questions, but he could give her no answer except 'yes'; and 'no'. His mind was sick.

The next morning, Netramani saw that Chhakadi was not in the house. He did not return that afternoon or that evening. She sent out several people in search of him, but he was not found.

But Chhakadi had not gone anywhere—he had seated himself in the doorway of Gouranga Sena's house at Haripur and had not moved at all.

Dama saw his uncle sitting quietly outside the house and ran in to his mother. "Bou!" he shouted out, "*Dadi* is here!"

Baraju came out and saw Chhakadi sitting there quietly. "Why are you sitting here?" he said. "Come inside!" He took him into the house.

When they were inside the house, Baraju asked, "What brought you here, Chhakadi?"

And Chhakadi said in a low voice, "I will go!"

"Go where?" Baraju asked.

"Wherever you go!"

Tears rained from his eyes in large drops.

"Shame on you, crybaby! Be a man, little brother!"

GLOSSARY

adharma the absence of *dharma* (moral principles) (see *dharma*)

agnya literal meaning: "I am at your command!" (*Agnya* is used as a mark of respect while addressing a person who is older or of higher rank

amala a government official of low or middle rank

ambula the dried seed of a mango, used to add a sour taste to curries

amina a surveyor of land working for the government

arisa pitha a kind of fried sweet made from powdered grains and brown sugar

arua rice which has not been parboiled after the husk is removed (see *usna*)

aswin Hindu month corresponding to October

baap re! a Hindi expression literally meaning "Oh my father!" which supposedly expresses awe or wonder but often has no meaning

babu a respectable middle-class gentleman (The word was originally used by the British in colonial times to refer to Indian clerks employed by the East India Company)

babugiri the genteel lifestyle typically adopted by a *babu*

baidya an apothecary (practitioner of the ancient Hindu system of medicine)

bandobast an operation carried out by revenue officials to survey land and update land records

badi a kind of savoury cake made from lentils and rice, ground into a paste and left to dry in the sun. Used as a condiment.

batua a small pouch made of cloth

bauri a very low caste in Odisha

bedi the platform on which the bride and bridegroom are seated during a wedding ceremony *beeda* the triangular shape into which a betel leaf (paan) is folded before it is put inside the mouth

bhai bou the wife of one's younger brother

bhandaruni a female barber, whose services are required at every Odia wedding

bhauja the wife of one's elder brother

biri the seeds of a kind of leguminous plant, also known as *urad* or blackgram, used for making *daal* as well as *pithas* (cakes)

bishtu colloquial form of 'Vishnu', the Supreme God. (*Please refer to "Notes".*)

bohu daughter-in-law

bou mother or "mother of" (the word often forms part of a woman's name, e.g. *Hara Bou* = mother of Hara)

chaka a large plot of land which has not been divided into smaller plots

chakhanda the width of the human palm, from the tip of the thumb to the tip of the little finger

chandaala a person born into a very low caste who is doomed to perform humiliating occupations such as scavenging

chasa someone who belong to the peasant caste

chatshali village school

Chhi! ('shame on you') an expression indicating disgust or disapproval

chuaan an oily substance prepared from tobacco leaves

chooda flattened and dried rice flakes, used as a snack

chowkidaar a watchman responsible for the security of the village

chowkidaari a committee formed to oversee the security of the village

cowrie the shell of a kind of mollusc, formerly used as a unit of money of low value

dadi colloquial form of "dada" (father's younger brother)

dakshina money paid to a Brahmin priest for performing a religious ritual

dalal a broker or agent who acts on behalf of someone

dandabat the act of prostrating one's body on the ground to show respect

dedhsura the elder brother of one's husband

dharma (i) religion (ii) virtue (iii) morality (the moral code that one is expected to live by)

dhania (coriander) a spice derived from the seeds of a plant

dhenki a heavy, lever-like implement operated with the foot, used to pound rice

diara the younger brother of one's husband (Traditionally, married Hindu women treat a *diara* as a friend, which whom jokes, often of a ribald nature, can be exchanged.)

domb a person from a very low caste

ekadashi the eleventh day in the dark fortnight of the moon, which is considered auspicious

gamuchcha a coarse hand-spun and hand-woven towel

ghaat the stone steps on the bank of a river or pond which lead to the water

gina a small metal bowl

gooda molasses (coarse brown sugar made from sugarcane juice)

gua-kati a nutcracker used to crack open areca nuts for use in paan

gunia a witch-doctor

gumashta a clerk employed by a land-owning zamindar

haat village market

haath the length of the human forearm from finger-tip to elbow, commonly adopted as a unit of measurement of length

hakima a judge or magistrate or a highly placed government official *hakimi* the qualities, specially of arrogance, possessed by a 'hakima'

halahal a deadly poison, believed to have come out of the sea, which was consumed by the god Shiva (Mahadev) in order to save all living creatures from its lethal effects

haladi turmeric (the bright-yellow root of a plant) used as a spice as well as a cosmetic or astringent

handi a small earthenware vessel used for cooking

jaa sister-in-law (the wife of the brother of one's husband)

janhi ridge-gourd (a vegetable belonging to the cucurbit family)

jatra a village opera

juhhar the act of bowing one's head, with palms joined together, to show respect

kaali mati literal meaning : "black earth". (*Please refer to "Notes"*)

kali kaala the Evil Age, which comes at the end of a cosmic cycle

kantha a bed-spread or mattress made by patching together the remnants of old garments

kapala the literal meaning is 'forehead'. One's destiny (karma) is supposedly inscribed at the time of birth into the lines etched in the forehead *kapota* dove

karma one's fate or destiny, supposed to have been pre-determined by the good as well as evil deeds that one has performed during earlier births

khadu a gold bracelet worn by a woman

khai a sweet made from puffed rice and molasses

khala an open yard in which harvested crops are stored

khatuli a little bed in which the image of a deity is laid to rest at night

khiri sweet pudding prepared from rice and milk, served at the end of a meal

khoodi aunt (the wife of the younger brother of one's father) *khuda* the husk (seed-cover) obtained from grains of rice, used as cattle-feed

kolatha a kind of coarse lentil generally fed to cattle

kora a sweet made from grated coconuts

mahajan money-lender

maichia a person who is effeminate in behavior or who lacks the toughness expected of a man and is therefore looked down upon as being less than a man. (The word can be an insult or a mild, affectionate reproach.)

mamlatkaar a person who exercises some authority and meddles in the affairs of others by virtue of his position

manisha-pania the essential qualities of a good human being

mattha a monastery

mathia an earthenware vessel of small or medium size used to store water

mohura a kind of traditional Odia curry

mohurir a lawyer's clerk

moodhi fluffy puffed rice, consumed as a snack

mooga (moong) a kind of lentil (leguminous plant) used to make *daal*

murabi guardian (the person in a family who is most widely respected and obeyed)

mulia an agricultural labourer, often landless

nani elder sister

paan the leaf of the betel plant, to which slaked lime, crushed areca nut, catechu and fragrant spices have been added

pakhala cooked rice soaked (often overnight) in water, eaten cold

panchana a whip used to drive bullocks

panchayat a group of respected elders (traditionally supposed to consist of five members) which administers justice in a village

piyada a messenger or servant of low rank

punya virtue earned through good deeds

ram leela a village opera narrating the story of Ram

saaga greens (small plants whose leaves are cooked and eaten)

sajana the drum-stick tree or its fruit

sana bohu the younger daughter-in-law in a family

sankha thick bangles made out of white conch-shell, which indicate that the wearer is married and that her husband is living

santhula a lightly spiced vegetable curry

sasu mother-in-law

shika a small rope basket, slung from the ceiling of the kitchen, used to keep food out of the reach of children as well as domestic animals

sindura bright-red metallic powder which is considered sacred and is extensively used in Hindu rituals. *Sindura* worn in the parting of a woman's hair indicates that she is married and that her husband is living

tampa a kind of vicious venomous snake

tapasya fasting or other form of physical austerity performed by one who is seeking spiritual growth or enlightenment

theka turban (a covering for the head)

toka boy or young man

tulasi the sacred basil plant, revered by Hindus

turani water in which cooked rice has been soaked, to be eaten as *pakhala*

usna rice which has been parboiled and retains a portion of the husk

NOTES

1. These unpalatable names were supposed to protect her children from the jaws of death. (Chapter 1, page 3)

Uneducated Hindus in Odisha believe that a person with a name that carries an unpleasant meaning is rejected by Yama, the god of Death. Parents often, therefore, give their children such unpalatable names as Hagara (someone who suffers from perpetual diarrhoea), as a protection against premature death.

2. "Let him go to *Kalimati* or to Calcutta..." (Chapter 1, page 8)

Poor agricultural labourers from Odisha, usually landless, were forced to migrate to distant places in the north, particularly Punjab, in search of employment. They generally underwent a lot of suffering in these places and lived in dread of them. 'Kalimati' literally means 'an evil place where even the soil has turned black'.

3. "And now, you find *dedhsura* and *bhai bou* together in the same room! *Chhi, chhi*!" (Chapter 4, page 19)

In conservative Hindu families, a married woman is supposed to keep herself veiled when her *dedhsura* (husband's elder brother) is present, as a mark of respect. The *dedhsura* too is supposed to avoid looking at his *bhai bou* (younger brother's wife). Any violation of this tradition is frowned upon.

4. "*Bishtu*!" the younger *bohu* exclaimed apologetically..." (Chapter 4, page 20)

On accidentally touching someone with one's foot, one is expected to pronounce the name of Vishnu as a form of apology, since the human body is supposed to be a temple created by God.

